Wolf Man

Blue Rock Shifters: Book 5
By: Lynn Leite

By Lynn Leite

This is a work of fiction. Names, characters, places and incidents are the product of the author's imagination or are used fictitiously, and any resemblance to actual persons living or dead events or locals is purely coincidental.

By Lynn Leite

1

One week ago

For the first time in months, Aya was leaving the Bed and Breakfast for something other than a short hike in the woods. Of course, a guard was driving them. Jett, that day's appointed guard, was in the Driver's seat with Ellery. Aya was in the back seat with Blythe and three-year-old Gwen was strapped in a car seat between them. The third seat in the truck was occupied by Aya's longtime friend, Tasha.

Aya and Tasha had sort of insisted on being included in the trip to check on Emerald. They had met Emerald weeks ago when she came to the home they were currently occupying. The woman was the single mother of Gwen and the Assistant to the local mayor.

By Lynn Leite

Aya had assumed that was why Emerald was privy to the fact that the women at the Bed and Breakfast were part of the Witness Protection Program.

Aya still wasn't sure what it was that her friend Eve went through or how that had put her and her other two friends, Tasha and Ellery, in danger. The facts were sketchy, but there was one thing she knew for sure. Aya had been dying in the hospital's ICU Unit before they were brought to the Bed and Breakfast they now had as temporary housing. For whatever reason, Tasha and Ellery were also on death's door in the same facility before their friend Eve sent help. Now, they were living in a beautiful, old Victorian waiting for permanent housing.

Ellery had already hooked-up with one of the guards, so did another of rescued women named Jazz.

Aya might not know the whole story, but she had been dying and, now, she was healthy, living in a quaint town in the middle of nowhere. She'd take the middle of nowhere over dying any day.

Emerald had become a friend. In the months they had been there, she came to visit them often. When Aya and the others heard she had been attacked, they worried. Ellery had brought Emerald's three-year-old, Gwen, to stay with them for two nights because Emerald was recovering from an attack. What kind of attack it was hadn't been explained?

"Will you look at this place. How does an Assistant to the Mayor afford a place like this?" Aya glanced at Tasha, giving her a scolding look. Her comment was rude but true. The house wasn't a house. It was an estate.

Helping to unstrap Gwen from the confines of her car seat, the three-year-old bolted for the door.

Emerald waited for the toddler in the doorway of her home with Nico, the Deputy Mayor, by her side. Nico was familiar to the women at the safe house. He had been dubbed "Tall, dark, and dangerous" by one of the other women that currently resided at the old Victorian.

By Lynn Leite

The man exuded strength. It was more than just the kind you would expect from a public figure. All of the men that Aya had met since being part of the program were good looking and physically fit. She had met mostly men who were assigned to protect the women. The Security force in this tiny town seemed more like a Military unit than a local Police force. Aya wasn't complaining. They were all nice to look at and made the women feel safe. The Mayor explained that they would be on duty around the clock until they were sure no one was looking for them.

Gwen greeting her mother was understandable. What made Aya curious was Gwen calling Nico Daddy.

As far as she had heard, the man had more than one woman he was involved with. She also was sure that Emerald had told them that Gwen's father was never in the picture.

The toddler gave Nico the picture she drew of a "Wolf shipper". Aya wasn't sure what the picture was of since the three-year-old had only drawn a wobbly, oval body, four stick legs, and a stick neck with a circle on top. It could have been any animal, or maybe a spider.

They had heard everything about her Daddy being a shipper, whatever that meant. The Wolf part was probably because Gwen had gotten a hold of the book they had on Local Legends. Werewolves, ghosts, and several other weird happenings were rumored to be in the surrounding forest.

As soon as Nico went with Gwen to hang her masterpiece on the fridge, Tasha pounced.

"Alright, spill," Tasha said, glancing behind Emerald to make sure that Nico was gone.

"Spill?" Emerald asked, looking confused.

"Since when is Tall, dark and, dangerous Gwen's Daddy?" Tasha pulled no punches.

"It's a recent occurrence. We sort of eloped," Emerald explained.

"Sort of?" Aya tilted her head, waiting for more. Nico's reputation was not stellar and Emerald seemed like a smart woman.

"Yes," she blushed.

"That's why one of his ex's attacked you?" Aya had heard that it was because one of Nico's obsessed fans had seen Emerald as a threat. It made more sense now that some random woman had targeted the Mayor's Assistant.

"Apparently, she didn't take the news well," Emerald shrugged like it was no big deal.

Aya knew there was more to the story, but she also knew it wasn't really her business.

"How are you feeling?"

"I am much better now, thank you."

While Nico watched the three-year-old, Emerald took Tasha, Aya, and Ellery up the stairs for a tour of their home. Ellery had been right. Emerald had inherited the home from a distant relative. Emerald smiled as she explained that some parts of the home were still being renovated. The kitchen and a few other modifications had taken priority.

The bathroom in the hallway was one of the upgraded rooms and Aya's favorite. It was gorgeous: two sinks, a shower, a jacuzzi, and a privy wall for the toilet, all with a huge picture window overlooking the forest.

"This is my idea of a bathroom. Do you think we could order one like this to be put in the houses they are renovating?" Tasha was playing with the shower, going through all the different settings.

"I don't know, but it won't hurt to ask," Aya smiled.

Ellery and another of those in the Protection Program, Jazz, were already living on the site that Aya and Tasha would live on along with the others in the program.

The Mayor had chosen an abandoned group of homes that had been vacant since a storm nearly wiped out five of the seven homes. The program was gifting each of them a small home. Aya wasn't going to complain about that at all. A home on a lake in the middle of nowhere was her dream retirement. Now, because her friend Eve got mixed up with some nut and she and her other two friends were dragged into it somehow, Aya was getting her dream early.

"We should catch up with Ellery and Emerald," Aya suggested.

They found the other two women wrestling a window shut in one of the bedrooms.

"Have you seen all of the other rooms?" Ellery whipped her head around as soon as Aya and Tasha entered.

"We didn't want to be rude and explore on our own," Aya smiled.

"Feel free to go. I'm trying to shut all of these windows," Emerald said while moving down the row of windows.

By Lynn Leite

"It does smell sort of skunky." The odor was faint but getting stronger.

2

The hallway was wide and had dark paneling on either side. Each of the doors on either side held a surprise behind. Gwen's room was obvious. The Princess themed bedroom was a dead giveaway. It was probably the envy of every three-year-old girl in town.

The next room was the Master. A bathroom the same size as the one in the hallway was a surprise. Two glorious bathrooms in one home was a real luxury. Aya and Tasha were crossing to the bedroom next door to the Master and one of those windows was cracked open. The scent of skunk was already in the room.

"Tash, help me with this," Aya struggled with the older window. Generations of paint layers made it hard to close. They both pressed hard on the top, clicking it into place, when they noticed a woman on the lawn. Emerald's voice was now coming from below them and she was yelling at the woman.

"Oh no, she didn't," Tasha said with her eyes glued to the woman near the tree line.

"You think that's the woman that attacked Emerald?"

"She looks…" Tasha didn't finish the sentence or the thought.

What happened next was something they would never forget. It put into question everything they believed.

Emerald ran toward the woman faster than a woman who had been attacked days ago should be able to move. She took a flying leap and transformed. Clothing exploded off of her and a charcoal gray wolf landed where Emerald should have landed.

"Aya!" Tasha gasped as the woman they first saw also turned into a lighter gray wolf.

"Oh shit, Tash."

Neither of them knew what to say. The Emerald wolf was winning. The fight was practically over before it began. The darker wolf had the other one pinned down. Nico's voice was saying something, but they couldn't quite make out what it was since the window was now shut.

"There's more," Tasha pointed to the tree line where a giant man with the body of a god emerged with a huge black wolf at his side. He just strolled onto the lawn like it was no big deal to bring your pet wolf to a werewolf fight.

That's what they were, werewolves.

"Tash, the attack that Emerald had…"

"Shush, we'll talk about this later. We say nothing until we figure this out."

"It's a deal. Oh my god," Aya put her hand over her mouth.

"Now what? "Tasha's head whipped back toward the action.

The wolf with the god like giant turned into someone they knew, a very naked someone.

"Ghost," Tasha breathed as the man and his companion came and dragged the pinned wolf into the woods and disappeared.

Ghost was actually a man named Vaughn, who was Jazz's boyfriend or fiancé. They were living together in one of the renovated cabins being rebuilt for the women.

"Do you think she knows?"

"I don't know what to think," Aya shrugged.

The last part of this unnatural scene made Tasha's eyes go wide and Aya even more confused.

Their friend Ellery, the friend that they met in third grade, the one that, along with Eve, made up the four musketeers in High school, was running out to the lawn and handing Emerald, who was back to human and naked, a pile of clothing.

So many questions, so many emotions ran through Aya's head. Ellery had always believed in the paranormal. She was enlightened, some would say. Others would call her nutty. She had believed it possible that the books at the B&B could be true. She believed that werewolves were real, that ghosts roamed the forest, and that witches danced in the moonlight.

"Why wouldn't she tell us?" Tasha had apparently believed her eyes and had seen their friend running clothing to Emerald, the werewolf.

Had the attack from the mystery woman been a bite that made Emerald different? What about Ghost, since when is he part wolf?

"Tasha, we wouldn't have believed her if she had told us. Maybe, she did and we didn't listen."

"How come she knows?"

"Beats me, I'm not even sure what that was."

"Should we ask Ellery?"

"No, maybe it's a secret. What if they don't like the fact that we know?" Aya shook her head.

"I don't know anything except that I just saw the impossible."

"Maybe, Nico doesn't really invest in the Shipping company that he said he did?"

Both of them connected the dots. Gwen wasn't saying Wolf shipper. She was saying Wolf shifter.

As soon as Gwen had said it was a Wolf shipper like Daddy, the man had offered an explanation. The three-year-old mistaking the word shipper for shifter was becoming more likely.

"You are right. We should wait. For now, we say nothing, we act normal, and we investigate," Aya's voice was barely a whisper.

"Right, who knows who might be one?" Tasha agreed, nodding her head. "Do you think we are safe?"

"I trust Ellery, who apparently knows about this. She would never stick around or let us stay if we were in trouble."

"You are right. Maybe, she's not the fruit loop we all thought she was."

"Only you thought she was a fruit loop, Tasha."

"I always told Ellery that I'd need to see it to believe it. Now, I've seen it and I'm not sure what to believe."

"I'm not sure either, but I am curious. Maybe, we should re-read those books that Alice brought to us."

"I didn't bother looking at them in the first place," Tasha admitted. "I'm going to look at them now. Was Alice trying to tell us without telling us?"

"She's the Mayor's wife. The Mayor probably knows. Nico knows. Apparently, Ellery knows too. Even the three-year-old has a clue."

"We could just ask."

"Sure, who are you suggesting we ask? We aren't supposed to know. Maybe, there is a reason for that."

"That's a good reason to say nothing?" Tasha looked at Aya, who generally had the voice of reason in most situations.

"For now, keep your eyes and ears open. We can snoop a little and find out who to ask and what to ask."

"You don't snoop. That's my job," Tasha grinned.

"You have a new partner in crime. Let's get downstairs. Remember, act like nothing is different."

"Sure, nothing, except for everything," Tasha laughed, hesitating at the top of the stairs.

"Tasha, I am sure that if they meant us harm, we would know by now," Aya said close to the woman's ear, hoping they could pull this off. Was pretending nothing was wrong the right thing to do? Aya had no idea.

3

Present day

"Don't go far," Jett called to Aya and Tasha. They were in sneakers and workout gear, stretching in the driveway.

The two women had taken up jogging in the last week. There wasn't enough man power to follow them and still patrol the forest.

The guards on the old Victorian had been reduced, due to a more urgent need on the Pack borders. Summer was in full swing and the Paranormal Investigators that normally booked a stay at Blythe's place were now camped in two different locations on Pack land. Making sure that the Paranormal groups and the women left at the B&B didn't stumble on a young shifter out for a run was getting harder.

"Why shouldn't we go far? Is there something dangerous out on the road?" Tasha barked back.

Jett shook his head. Aya and Tasha had been acting strange, whispering to each other, staring at the guards that still made their rounds at the B&B. He was starting to think they might have seen what happened at Emerald and Nico's place with Cora. They didn't say anything. They were just acting suspicious.

"No, Tasha, this road just leads to a more dangerous road, a road with a lot more cars on it. There was a bear sighting across town, but you should be fine," Jett said intentionally, trying to keep them close to home.

"A bear?" Tasha's eyes widened.

"He's joking, You are joking, right?" Aya looked at Jett for a real answer.

"Aya, we are in the forest. There are bears. The likely hood of you and Tasha encountering one on your run is slim but not zero."

"What about wolves?" Aya asked, giving Jett the first indication that they might know more than they are saying.

"We have those too and coyotes, plus the occasional fisher cat."

"What's a fisher cat?" Tasha asked

"It's basically a mean weasel with sharp teeth. They make a sound like a person screaming. They hardly ever come out during the day. It shouldn't be an issue."

"Now, you're messing with me.," Tasha rolled her eyes.

"No, I'm not, look it up."

"I will," Tasha huffed.

"We will be back in time to change for dinner. Come on, Tasha," Aya said, yanking on her friend's arm. Tasha was stubborn and would argue with Jett all day if she had the chance.

They jogged maybe a half mile before Tasha spoke.

"Do you think that Jett was making it up?"

"Making what up?" Aya asked. "There are bears in the woods. He didn't flinch when we said wolf."

"The cat thing.

"Fisher cat."

"That's it. A mean weasel with sharp teeth that sounds like a person screaming?" Tasha asked.

"Tasha, we saw three people turn from human to wolf and you're questioning the existence of a mean weasel."

"Jazz's man went from wolf to human, a very naked human. No wonder the girl was all over the man."

"Get your head out of the gutter, Tasha. We both saw exactly the same thing. We have to believe it's real."

"Werewolves are real. So, why didn't Ellery mention it? For years, she's been trying to say witches and fairies are real, among other things. Why wouldn't the girl jump at the chance to tell us werewolves are real?"

"We have gone over this. Even if she did, we would have ignored her. She spouts stuff like this all the time."

"This time it's real."

"Exactly, so why not the fisher cat thing Jett mentioned?"

"You have a point. I was reading one of the books that Alice brought about Local legends. It was called Werewolf 101. I thought it was a joke. It's a handwritten journal that was in with the other books," Tasha admitted as they ran at a slow pace.

Neither of them was a runner. They had taken up the sport so they could talk without anyone overhearing at the B&B. Between Blythe, Mary Grace, and Sarina, there's usually someone nearby. The guards outside were sometimes hidden, so taking a run is the only thing they can do to assure no one overheard.

"What did it say?"

"Standard Werewolf stuff."

"Oh, right I know so many standard Werewolf things. I'm not Ellery, Tasha. I know only what I see in the movies and those facts conflict." Aya was at a loss on what to do about what they had seen.

"I think, eventually, we need to talk to Ellery. She's the one that brought clothing to Emerald, like it was normal for Emerald to burst out of her Human skin and turn into a dog."

"A wolf, Tasha, I think that calling her a dog might seem offensive."

"Try not to offend the werewolves. Got it."

"What did the journal say?"

"I only got to the second page and Blythe came in."

"Do you think she knows?" Aya asked.

"She is from here. Maybe, it's a town secret that there are a few werewolves in town."

"We know Ghost is one of them. We know that Nico's ex is one. She probably bit Emerald and she ended up turning into a wolf."

"How do we know that? Emerald might always have been one. Maybe, the guards aren't for our protection as much as they are to protect the town secret," Tasha said as they got to the main road.

"That actually makes sense."

"Don't act so surprised," Tasha snapped.

"I still don't know if it's a great idea to just come out and ask. If Ellery is keeping the secret for a reason, I don't want to pressure her."

"Maybe, Eli told her. He is Head of Security. He must know or maybe he is one. Jazz's man is a wolf. Who do you think the other guy was with him?"

"The giant god-like man that looked like he had a pet wolf?"

"Yes, him."

"I don't know, Tasha. I was with you, remember? Maybe, they will be at dinner tonight. I'm sure Jazz was invited."

The women at the B&B were invited to Emerald and Nico s place for dinner. Emerald had said she felt like a bad host the last time they were there.

Aya and Tasha didn't mention that they understood she was busy getting attacked by a werewolf in the yard at the time.

"I don't know if I'm going to be able to act normal, Aya."

"Why, because Emerald is a wolf now? The woman was attacked. She needs support, not prejudice."

"Prejudice?" Tasha croaked as they turned around to go back home.

"Yes, against werewolves, Emerald is good people and Ghost might look terrifying, but he loves Jazz and has kept us safe. Other than the crazy ex-girlfriend, we haven't had any indication that they are dangerous."

"Fine, I will judge each werewolf I meet individually, on their personality. The big question is how do I know who is wolf and who is not? It's not like we ever saw this before, and we have lived here for months."

"We have lived here at the B&B, isolated for months. We need to snoop a little, take a few long walks in the forest," Aya stated.

"Looking for shifters seems like a bad idea."

"Do you have a better one? I need more information to assure that we are not going insane together."

"I still say we just ask Ellery."

"I don't want to put her in that position until I know for sure that what we saw was real. If it's a secret she's not supposed to tell, then she'd be torn between telling us and lying to keep the secret. That is if it's real."

By Lynn Leite

"If it wasn't real, we are in bigger trouble than I thought."
"You are right about that."

4

"You're driving us?" Aya saw Jett leaning against one of two cars waiting out front.

"I am driving some of you. I was also invited to dinner. Do you have a problem with that?"

"I just thought you'd be off duty."

"I'm off duty going to dinner at Nico and Emerald's. I don't live far from here, so I offered to drive. Cole can't drive two cars."

"Cole is the only one on duty today?"

"Aya, you have all been here for months. It's safe. I doubt you even need guards here, other than the fact that you tend to get in trouble at times."

"I have never been in trouble."

"I was thinking more about what happened with Jazz."

"She got a husband out of it or, at least, it seems to be heading in that direction."

"Are you looking for a husband, Aya?" Jett sounded genuinely curious.

"Looking, no, not really, are you?"

"I don't think a husband would suit my taste," Jett grinned, making Aya giggle like an idiot. She wasn't a giggler, but the men in this town made woman do stupid things just by looking at them.

"Wife, Jett, are you looking for a wife?"

"Yes." The clear answer, with no hesitation, shocked Aya.

"Oh well, that's not what I expected."

"Who wouldn't want what Jazz and Ghost have, or Nico and Emerald?"

"What about Eli and Ellery?"

"Your friend was the answer to Eli's dreams. It was a pleasure to watch him fall. Most men want a partner, Aya. We just don't start planning our weddings at the age of six."

"I can honestly say I have no wedding planned."

"Neither do I. It's a waste of money."

"I thought you just said that you wanted a wife."

"You don't have to have a wedding to have a wife. It's the life that comes after the ceremony that is the true test."

"I had no idea you were so deep," Aya smiled, seeing the others coming out to join them.

"I'm the whole package. Looks, smarts, I have a good job…"

"And a big ego."

"Nothing wrong with knowing your worth. You could say the same. You are beautiful, smart…"

"Unemployed and on the run from an unknown threat," Aya finished for him.

"As I said, I think it is just a matter of time before you can relax. Blake is confident that you are all safe to live your life here without being guarded."

"I hope so."

"We already reduced the security."

"I noticed. Who will you flirt with when you're not guarding us?" Aya teased. All of the guards flirted with all of the women and most of the women flirted back.

"I have been very professional. Mary Grace is the flirt. I just smile and nod."

"It wasn't a judgment, Jett. I, for one, like a little flirting now and then."

"I will keep that in mind," Jett said, opening the back door for her as the others piled into the two vehicles.

Tasha's sideways look as they rode to Emerald's told Aya that the woman had something to say.

"What?" Aya whispered.

"I saw you," Tasha smirked.

"You saw me what, talking to Jett? Guilty as charged."

"You were doing more than talking," she hissed. Aya could swear she saw Jett smile in the rear-view mirror. Tasha's voice was barely a whisper, but it seemed Jett heard at least part of their conversation.

"We can talk later." Aya used a warning tone.

"I wasn't judging. He is perfect for you."

This time, Aya was sure she saw Jett smile.

"Would you stop," Aya said a little louder. There was no point whispering if he could hear her.

A thought occurred to her as Tasha went silent.

Jett shouldn't be able to hear them. It was possible he would know they were whispering but not what was said. Aya was often the designated driver when the four friends used to go out. She could never actually hear what was being said unless the women in the back leaned over the front seat and spoke in an elevated tone.

"You have that look on your face," Tasha said.

"What look?"

"The look you get when you're trying to solve a puzzle."

"Life is a puzzle, Tasha." Aya realized how lame that sounded and laughed.

The car that Aya and Tasha were in arrived first as the vehicle driven by Cole pulled in next to them seconds later. Mary Grace jumped out, having the same reaction to Emerald's home that Tasha and Aya had the week before. The Manor house was looking even nicer than it had just days ago. The shudders looked freshly painted. The brick façade had been power washed. The grounds were trimmed as well.

Eloping with the assistant Mayor had upgraded Emerald's love life as well as her home. Aya tried not to think about what else it had done to Emerald.

"This place is huge," Mary Grace gaped.

"Weird that it's in the middle of nowhere like this," Sarina added.

"Oh, please, everything in this town is the middle of nowhere. I think it's perfect, no neighbors to bother you," Tasha commented.

"Hey, we are all going to live at the lake. We will be your neighbors," Mary Grace whined.

"Like I said," Tasha looked at Mary Grace, "some neighbors can be annoying."

"What did I do?"

"Nothing yet," Tasha barked.

"Tasha, lay off Mary Grace. Mary Grace, Tasha is just being difficult. If any of us are going to be hard to live with, it's her and she knows it," Aya glared at Tasha.

She knew her friend was joking around with Mary Grace, but Mary Grace didn't.

"I was kidding, Mary Grace. If you really annoyed me, you'd know it."

"On that note, would you all like to come inside?" Emerald called from the top step.

"Yes, thank you," Sarina said, quickly dragging Mary Grace behind her.

"She's sensitive. You have to be more careful."

"Her low self-esteem isn't my problem."

"Yes, it is. We all are in the same boat."

"The boat is sinking," Tasha glanced around.

"Keep your voice down. I swear that Jett could hear our entire conversation on the way here."

"The one where I said that you were flirting with him?"

"Yes, that one, I like Jett. I like Cole and Parker too. Jenkins is pushy and annoying. Elliot, I don't know all that well, and Susanne and June are fast becoming friends."

"So, Jett and Cole, huh?"

"I was trying to get to know him, maybe see what he knows," Aya hissed. She hadn't really been doing that, but she knew that Tasha wasn't going to let it go.

"Oh, good idea."

Aya sighed in relief. Tasha was like a dog with a bone, relentless.

5

"Sir, I'm starting to think it is possible that Aya and Tasha know something," Jett informed Eli.

"What makes you think that?"

"Ever since the incident last week, they are acting suspicious, long walks alone, whispering. Blythe said they were looking at the books a bit more intently."

"They were upstairs here in the house when Cora attacked. Am I right?"

"Yes, Sir, they were taking a tour of the home when Cora arrived. I don't know what, if anything, they saw, but I do know they are acting differently."

"Alright, keep me posted. I will have Ellery talk to them and see if she can determine if they saw anything. In the meantime, keep your ears open."

"It would be easier if they all knew."

"Yes, it would," Eli nodded as the house filled with more and more people.

"I thought this was just dinner?" Aya noticed the guards had showed up as well as the Mayor and his wife, Alice.

"It is dinner, but since Emerald and Nico eloped, their friends decided to make it sort of a reception," Jett said from behind her.

The man wasn't there a moment ago, making his being there now suspicious.

"Jett, let me ask you something. Did you hear Tasha and I talking in the car?"

"About flirting?"

"You did hear us, how?"

"I have very good hearing. It wasn't intentional."

"When people, women especially, whisper, it's to keep other people from hearing."

"You didn't want me to know we were flirting?"

"We were not flirting. We were talking about flirting. There is a difference."

"I see. I will try not to overhear your whispering in the future."

"And I will try not to discuss personal things with you or near you."

"Aya, you can ask me anything."

"And you'd answer truthfully?"

"Yes."

"I will keep that in mind." Aya wasn't sure what she would even ask. *"Hey Jett, what's your take on the Werewolf legend,* or *"Jett, did you notice two women changing into wolves on the lawn the other day*? Maybe, *"Jett, you wouldn't happen to be one of them, would you?"* She needed the right question so she didn't look insane or get in trouble for knowing some super-secret that no one wanted to get out.

"You have that look again," Tasha laughed as she came to stand with Aya. "the solving life's puzzle one."

"I'm trying to decide what to do."

"About the sexy guard you insist you are not flirting with?"

"Yes, among other things."

"So, you're admitting you are flirting with Jett."

"I admit I am chatting with him and there might be a little innocent flirting between us. He heard us in the car."

"So, we didn't talk about you know what?"

"I know, but we were whispering."

"So, that probably means that he has good hearing."

"I'm overthinking. Let's mingle."

"Right," Tasha nodded.

"And stop staring. If I noticed, others will."

"It's hard not to."

"I know."

A commotion in the Living room drew the attention of everyone. Aya stood on tip-toes to see over the people in front of her. Ellery was surrounded by the crowd. Her head bowed and she was crying. Aya was just about to rip through the wall of people, mostly guards, who had come to the impromptu party to get to her friend. That's when she noticed Eli was down on one knee with a ring in hand, facing her.

"Tasha, look, he is proposing."

"Who is proposing? I thought they eloped," Tasha said, craning her neck.

"Not Nico, Eli. He is proposing to Ellery."

"I'm not surprised. Do you see the way he looks at her, sort of like… you know?"

"If you say sort of like the way Jett looks at me, I will put Nair in your shampoo."

"I was going to say the way Ghost looks at Jazz," Tasha smirked.

Aya knew that wasn't what Tasha was going to say. She was just good at quick thinking.

"Nice save. Speaking of Ghost, his giant friend is here," Aya gestured to the Greek god on the far side of the Living room.

"His name is Chance and he is Ghost's brother."

"Oh, you've done some investigating?" Aya laughed.

"Jazz told me. Do you think that he is one of the...?"

"Hold that thought," Aya slammed her hand across Tasha's mouth, seeing Emerald approaching. "Thank you for inviting us. This is some party," she smiled.

"It is turning out to be. I'm sorry I was such a mess last week."

"You weren't yourself," Tasha said before Aya could stop her.

"You can say that again. I feel much better now."

"Nico has something to do with that, I assume."

"He does. Feel free to wander. I think you know most of the people here."

"Because they are our Security team, Emerald. You are the Assistant to the Mayor. Do you have any idea when he might deem it safe for us to live normally?"

"I have heard a rumor that by the end of the summer they believe it will be unnecessary for you to be guarded. You didn't hear that from me."

"Of course not," Aya smiled," I would like my life to go back to some sort of normal."

"Normal is overrated," Emerald glanced at Nico, who smiled from across the room.

"You're right. My life is far from normal and I have no complaints. One of my best friends just got engaged. We have new homes being prepared on a beautiful lake. Life is good, weird but good."

6

The party at Emerald and Nico's didn't give them any real answers to the questions they had hinted at. Asking about what they had seen was still a last resort. If they were not supposed to know or worse, if they had imagined it, asking could have consequences Aya wasn't ready for. Jett said he would tell Aya the truth. Ellery wouldn't lie if asked outright. Ellery and Nico had for sure seen what they had. The Wolf girl was Nico's ex or someone that he had dated. It was possible that Nico was a werewolf as well, but they had no way of telling. Assuming Jazz knew was a good bet, since her boyfriend was a wolf part-time. It still seemed so unreal.

"Alright, I have an idea?" Aya said a few days later as they stretched for their run.
"Should I be worried? Did it hurt your head?" Tasha chuckled at her own jokes.

"No, it didn't hurt, not yet," Aya put her hands on her hips to show her friend this was serious.

"Sorry, what's your idea?"

"Today, we should run that way," Aya pointed to the well-worn path in the woods.

"Into the forest, with the bears and the Cat things?" Tasha asked.

"Yes, I was thinking we would surprise Jazz and Ellery."

"Oh, and maybe we see a *ghost*?" Tasha was terrible at speaking code, but Aya knew they were on the same page.

If they accidently stumbled on a giant Black wolf in the forest and that giant Black wolf turned out to be a man, then they would have to tell them the truth.

"Yes, we are *ghost* hunting. The woods here are rumored to be haunted. According to the legends, right?"

"Right," Tasha grinned.

Aya had noticed that Jett was not on-duty that day. She always knew when he was on duty. It was like she could feel his eyes on her. She actually liked that he was watching her. Tasha teased her about flirting with Jett and Aya couldn't deny she was interested in that specific guard more than the others.

Parker was on the other side of the house and Jenkins, the man relieving him, was with him. If they were going to go in the opposite direction today, now was the chance. No one was watching. The two women ran the path until the house disappeared from view.

"Why does this feel like we are doing something wrong?" Tasha laughed as they slowed to a walk.

"I feel like we are sneaking out at night as teens, so our parents don't catch us."

"Exactly, they said when we first arrived that we should not go alone into the forest."

"We are not alone. I'm with you and you are with me."

"You have a point. So, which way is the lake?"

"The lake is that way, I think."

"You think? Aya, wasn't there a path the day we went to the lake and Ellery looked like she was drowning?" That had been weeks ago and Ellery was not drowning. She had just been startled

"That was because Parker frightened her. Did you see how quickly Eli swam out to save her?" Aya kept walking, so Tasha kept following.

"And the rest is history. I can't believe he proposed at Emerald's place, right in the middle of their sort of Elopement party."

"I like that she is happy. When we were all brought here because of whatever happened to Eve, I was glad to see she was happy too. We all deserve happiness."

"I wonder if Eve knows?"

"If Eve knows why we were put in Witness Protection?" Tasha asked.

"No, about werewolves being real."

"Good question, her husband, Kingston, is almost as big as Ghost."

"Speaking of which, do you think his brother will be there? Do you think he is a werewolf too?"

"Leave it to you to crush on the most terrifying man we have seen so far."

"Ghost was pretty terrifying."

"At first, but then he saved Jazz and she went from miserable to awesome. I think the lake is that way," Aya turned slightly to the right.

"I think we are getting lost."

"We are not lost, just taking the long way. I know for sure that the homes they are renovating are north of Blythe's place. The sun rises in the East and sets in the West, so we are going Northwest right now," Aya said, turning another quarter turn so they would be heading North.

"This is one of those times where you act like you know what you're doing but you really have no clue, isn't it?"

"I have a clue, Tasha. If you want to take over, be my guest."

"I just don't want to spend a night out here in the forest is all."

"We won't spend the night out here. Look, there's the old quarry."

"Why is the quarry on our right and not our left, like it was when we were at the lake?"

"It doesn't matter as long as we see the lake. We are going around the lake to the houses on the other side. This way might be a little longer, but we will get there"

"Alright, but if we get lost, no one even knows where we went, Aya."

"I will call for help if we get lost. I brought my cell phone just in case."

"Thank god for that. Now, all we need is reception. Do you know how big the lake actually is?"

"No."

"We should have probably thought this out before."

"We are fine, you'll see. If all else fails, we turn around and go home."

"You can find home?"

"Yes, Tasha, have some faith."

"I have faith in a lot of things you do, Aya. Wilderness survival isn't one of them."

"Shush, did you hear that?" Aya stopped in her tracks.

"Hear what, water I hope?"

"The lake is over there. I can see it through the trees. That's not what I'm talking about," Aya hissed, pointing to her left and the forest beyond. "Just listen, I hear voices."

Tasha strained to hear anything. The sound of a man's voice was faint.

"Hunter maybe?" Tasha offered in a hushed tone.

"Maybe, is hunting even allowed in these woods? What if Ghost is running and gets mistaken for…"

"For what a wolf? Now, we're not only okay with the idea of shifters being real. We are worried they might get hurt."

"Yes, Tasha, they are our friends. You talked to Emerald at the party like she was normal and you're after Ghost's brother, who is probably one."

"I'm not after him. I'm just fantasizing about him. That's different."

"Fine, keep fantasizing. My point is that this town is protecting them and the secret. Therefore, we should too."

"I agree. So, which way toward the lake, or toward the hunters?"

"That way," Aya pointed.

"I swear if I get shot out here," Tasha started.

"You won't. We won't get that close."

"Sure, because two girls from the suburbs with zero wilderness training can sneak up on a man who stalks his prey in the wild," Tasha groaned but followed in a crouch.

7

"What do you mean you haven't seen them? "Eli was trying to stay calm.

"I haven't seen them since I came on-duty."

"And you didn't think to tell us sooner, Jenkins." Jett had come to relieve Jenkins and get his report. So far, the reports, day after day, were the same. The women were fine, no sign of them discovering they lived in a Pack town. Today, Jenkins said that Sarina and Mary Grace were with Blythe, but he didn't know where Tasha or Aya had gone.

"Cole mentioned that they ran the road every day. I wasn't that worried."

"You have been on duty for four hours now. When was the last time you took a four-hour run?" Jett snapped. His level of concern was more than expected. He was sure that both women had seen something the other day. He wasn't sure why they would not mention it at all, but the way they acted lately was suspicious.

"I took a four-hour run yesterday, Sir," Jenkins answered.

"In Human form?" Eli barked.

"No, Sir."

"Exactly, they weren't on the road. We would have seen them and running the road, for them, takes only an hour at most. They went somewhere else.

"Jenkins, run the perimeter, see if you can pick up the scent," Eli ordered," in Human form," he added when the man started to remove his shirt.

"I'm calling Ghost. Maybe, they went that way to visit with Ellery," Eli added.

"Shouldn't you call Ellery then?" Jett asked Eli.

"No, if they aren't there, I don't want her worrying or worse, looking for them. There are two groups camped out on the far side of the quarry we are avoiding."

"Hunters?" Jett asked, hearing this for the first time.

"Not the gun toting kind. They are looking for Sasquatch, ghosts, anything rumored to be here in the forest."

"Great."

"It gets worse. Reed, Stockson's second over in the Moon Valley Pack, said that one of theirs was spotted by these people."

"They saw them shift?"

"No, they saw Damon shifted."

Damon had been turned when captured and experimented on, along with the others now living in Moon Valley. They were all found in a warehouse over a year ago. Damon and another of the rescued, Devlin, had not been exactly human when they were taken. They were what was referred to as Demons. Not the hell spawn kind, the kind that was basically a Vampire/Human hybrid. Vampires were extinct, but a small fraction of their children's grandchildren and great grandchildren still existed in secret, much like shifters did.

Damon, when turned, resembled the monsters depicted in the old legends: ridge back, partially upright, wicked teeth, more monster than wolf.

"Let me guess, they called in the troops," Jett shook his head.

"Apparently, just one glimpse of Damon, who ran as soon as he sensed them nearby, was enough to start a Witch hunt"

"You mean Sasquatch hunt. We have had those before."

"Two other camps were set up a day later. The two near the quarry are technically on our land."

"Great, so we can go kick them off?"

"Blake thinks kicking them off will make them think there's something here to hide."

"There is something here to hide."

"Leaving them where they are means we can keep an eye on them and intervene legally, if necessary."

"I hadn't thought of that. Eli, I am pretty sure that Aya and Tasha saw something when Cora showed up at Emerald's."

"Have they said anything yet?"

"No, not yet, but they didn't used to run every day. Tasha didn't run at all and, now, they are missing."

"You think they might be on a hunt of their own?" Eli looked worried.

"I think they might be looking for your mate actually. If they saw what happened then, they saw Ellery was there."

"They trust Ellery."

"Maybe, they are afraid to ask her?"

"I couldn't say what those two are thinking. I'm still working on figuring out my mate."

"They went down the path to the lake," Jenkins called from the entrance in the backyard.

"Alright, let's go."

"All of us, Sir?" Jenkins asked.

"Yes, you lost them. You can help find them. I don't care if your off-duty."

"Yes Sir, I just thought someone should stay behind and watch the others."

"You mean flirt with the others," Jett rolled his eyes. "You know as well as I do, they don't really need guards if they are in the house. No one is going to wander in there and shift for them. Out there, however, who knows what they could run into?" Jett's voice was accusatory.

"I like them."

"Good, so let's go and find the two you lost," Eli shook his head.

The three of them were nearly to the turn off that led to the lake when it became clear that Aya and Tasha didn't take the turn off. They kept going.

"Should we call for them?" Jenkins asked, scanning the forest.

"If we can't hear them, then they definitely can't hear us, Jenkins."

"Unless they aren't talking," Jenkins shrugged.

"Have you met Tasha?" Jett said sarcastically. "The more nervous she is, the more she talks. By now, they know they took a wrong turn."

The three were halfway up a ridge that overlooked the lake when the scents of the women stopped. All three had tracking experience, but this was a dead end.

Jett's heart was pounding. To their right was a sheer drop. It wasn't straight down but close enough.

"Jett, what's wrong?" Eli asked, sensing his concern. All of them were concerned, but Jett was near catatonic at the thought of the women falling.

"I can't look," he choked, his chest constricting, making it hard to breathe.

"Jett, is one of them…"

"I don't know." He liked all of the women at the safehouse. He hadn't honed in on anyone in particular until recently. He had spent more time watching and interacting with Tasha and Aya but chalked that up to his suspicion that they had seen more than they were saying.

Now, the thought of them injured or worse had his wolf pushing for the surface.

"They turned back. I can pick up the trail in the other direction," Jenkins said from just below the ridge.

"Jett, when we find them, you might want to figure out why you nearly lost control right now," Eli grinned. He wasn't angry. The man had just found his own mate but not before acting a bit erratic himself.

"I will, Sir."

"Good," Eli nodded, leaving the rest unsaid.

The reaction that Jett just had to the possibility of the women being injured was beyond concern. His feelings for one of them exceeded duty and friendship. He knew which of the two it was. He just hadn't seen it as anything serious until just now.

8

"You can't do that!" Tasha yelled, seeing what the two men in the woods were doing.

"So much for staying safely behind the trees," Aya groaned.

It was epically stupid to even get this close to two men in the wilderness. They were strangers with who knows what kind of rap sheet. Serial killers hunted and tortured little animals for fun and so did hunters as far as Aya was concerned. Hunting for food when starving was one thing. Hunting for sport was just wrong.

Aya had never really considered it wrong before this, if she had to be honest. As long as the hunter ate his kill and used the entire animal, she couldn't really object, despite it being something she was against personally. Now, with werewolves in the woods, she had a different take on it. What if Emerald was taking a run or Ghost? Those were the only two she was sure about, but it made sense that there were more.

"Where did you two come from?" one of the men stood.

"We came from none of your business," Tasha yelled. "You can't put traps out here."

"Who said?"

"I just did. This is Private property." Tasha had no clue if it was Private property or State land but, either way, Bear traps had to be illegal.

"The map says it's Town property and just over there is State," a weakly looking man came from behind the first one.

"People hike here and Bear traps are illegal."

"This is not a Bear trap," the first guy laughed. "We aren't looking for bear. If you knew what we were looking for, you'd be safe at home, with the doors bolted, instead of out here."

"Right, we know all about the ghosts and weird things rumored to be out here. If you are looking for ghosts, that's probably not going to work," Aya joined Tasha.

Upon closer look, she was sure that the men were not armed and Tasha was ex-military, in perfect fighting shape now that she started running again. These men were half the size of Jett and the other guards.

She wished Jett was there at the moment, but she wasn't as frightened as she had been when Tasha decided to confront them.

Aya couldn't see their camp anywhere in the forest, but she did see cameras and trip wires.

"You're filming some poor creature that walks into your trap. You're sick in the head. I'm getting the Rangers," Aya tugged on Tasha, who looked furious.

"We need proof when we catch Bigfoot."

"Seriously, Bigfoot, if he exists, has lived undetected for generations with only the occasional glimpse and sketchy reports. You think you two buffoons are going to not only trap him but get him on film?"

"Yes," one looked like they had just complimented them.

"Good luck surviving. I know if I stepped in that thing, I'd hunt down the guy that put it there. I think you two might be dead men walking, assuming that Bigfoot is real," Tasha was on a roll.

"That's only if you can catch him or her before the Rangers shut you down." Aya added.

"There's no law against us being here. We have a Camping permit."

"Well, I hope you have a Bear Trap permit to go with that."

"What do they know? Come on, Len, we have more traps to lay. I'd watch my step if I were you ladies," the weaselly one said, turning his back to them.

"If I step in one of those things, you will regret the day you were born, even if I have to beat the hell out of you with a bloody stump." Tasha was looking for a fight and Aya would have gladly watched if there hadn't been two of them.

"We have to go, Tasha."

"I'm warning you, take those down. If so much as a squirrel gets hurt, I'm coming back."

Aya grabbed a long stick for herself and one for Tasha.

"What's this for? Are we going back to beat them?"

"No, Tasha, if there are more traps out here, I'd rather not step in them. Do this." Aya poked the ground in front of her, using the stick. She looked like a blind person might, but the stick would trigger any other traps they came across in the denser foliage.

"Good idea."

"We need to tell the Mayor or someone," Aya said as they walked gingerly until they found a clear path.

"Blythe will know what to do, or one of the guards."

"Right," Aya said, walking at a quicker pace, hoping this was the right path. She had gotten turned around a little after the encounter with the two men.

"You're not going to yell at me for letting those men know we were there."

"Oh please, you could have taken them. I bet they are scientists, not real hunters. Blythe said she had a lot of that type stay at the house over the years."

"Those traps could snap a bear's leg. I hate to think what it would do to anything smaller."

"Like a wolf?"

"Yes, exactly like a wolf. I don't care how crazy we look. I need some answers."

"We can call Ellery when we get back."

"We could call her right now," Tasha said looking at Aya.

"Right, I forgot I brought my phone." Aya opened her phone and Jett's contact came up. She had recently programmed his number and it was the first to come up.

"You have Jett's number in your phone?" Tasha said when she saw his name on the screen.

"Don't start. You wanted to find Ghost's brother."

"I don't deny I was taken by the man. I'm a woman with wants and needs," Tasha laughed.

"So am I. Right now, we need help, and I want you to shut up so I can call."

9

"Where are you?" Jett said, not bothering with a greeting.

"Who is that?" Eli asked.

"It's *Aya*," he mouthed, still waiting for her to answer.

"*We are on a path in the forest.*"

"Which path?"

"*The one I hope leads back to Blythe's. We ran into some lovely gentlemen.*"

"Are you alright?" Jett asked, sensing that the gentlemen were not lovely at all. "I'm coming to you."

"NO*!*" Aya screamed. "*There are traps, Bear traps, well, at least one. and cameras.*"

"Shit," Eli groaned, hearing the conversation despite the fact that it wasn't on speaker.

"Can you describe where*?*"

"We were at the quarry when we realized we had gone too far and were on the wrong side of the lake. We turned around and were heading back, but we heard voices."

"So, you decided it was a good idea to investigate?"

"We thought they might be hunters and didn't want anyone or anything to get hurt," Aya said slowly. Jett could read between the lines. She knew something.

"You and I are going to have a talk about wandering off without anyone knowing."

"No, we aren't. I'm a grown woman and I brought a cell phone and Tasha with me. I'm tired of being watched, Jett. No one is after us. No one even knows we exist. We are safe, unless you'd like to tell me why we are not."

"I think you pissed her off," Jenkins said as they walked toward where they thought the women might be.

"Aya, how many traps did you see?" Eli called as they walked the path.

"One, definitely, but the men indicated there might be more."

"You spoke to them?" Jett yelled.

"I guess we know which one he is interested in," Jenkins said quietly.

"Shut up!" Jett yelled.

"I didn't get a chance to even answer. Why are you yelling?"

"It wasn't yelling at you, Aya. Answer the question."

"*Say please.*"

"Please, Aya, are you in danger?"

"*No, I think Tasha scared them.*" Jett heard a faint "*I did not*" from Tasha.

Jett's heart was pounding again. His wolf wanted to shift and chase after them to assure they were safe. They would definitely know for sure that shifters existed if he did.

"Aya, this is Eli. I need to know where you are, what you saw, and what was said."

"*We are currently on a path in the woods, headed... East, I hope. There were two men. They were putting out a Bear trap, a big one. Tasha sort of yelled at them and said it was illegal.*"

"It is illegal. What about the cameras? You said there were cameras."

"*The whole area just beyond where we were standing was booby-trapped. There were trip wires, cameras, motion detectors, and the Bear trap. They said they weren't hunting bear. Eli, they are hunting...*" Aya didn't have to say it.

"Anything paranormal."

"*Yes, that, they hinted that there were more traps out there and told us to watch our step.*"

"I will kill them," Jett was on the verge and the women, by the sound of it, were close.

"Jett, get a grip," Eli commanded. "Jenkins, put out a warning to the others. No running shifted until we eliminate the traps," Eli called to the third man.

A choaking sound and a whispered "*Oh my god*" coming from the phone Jett was holding meant the two women, or at least one of them, had heard that order.

"Aya, you still there?" Jett said glaring at his boss.

"*I'm… we're… Jett, I think I need that talk right now.*"

"I'm on my way."

"We are both on our way," Eli called as they started in the direction that they were sure the women were in. "Jenkins, you have your orders."

"Yes Sir," Jenkins turned, running back to the old Victorian at speeds that were clearly not human. They had come that way so there wouldn't be any traps.

"Sir, I think they know."

"I think they knew something already and I just affirmed it. How much or exactly what they know is to be determined." Eli took his cell out of the backpack they always wore when on duty. He called the one person that was going to make this better. "Ellery, we have an issue. Aya and Tasha know. I don't know how much, but they know."

"*I'll be right there,*" Ellery barked.

"No, we are coming to you. The woods aren't safe right now. I will explain when we get there."

"*Are they with you?*"

"Not yet. Oh, and I think Jett might have found his mate," Eli glanced at the man by his side.

"Tattletale," Jett growled but didn't deny it.

The urge to run to the women was strong. Watching every step to make sure there was no danger was tenuous. They patrolled the woods often. The chance that any of the hunters had made it in this far was slim to none. Still, they needed to be cautious.

"There they are." It was Tasha calling.

"Stay on the path and watch your step."

"You don't have to tell me. I don't want to lose a leg." Tasha was acting normal for Tasha. Aya was quiet and staring right at Jett.

"Ladies, I called Ellery. She's waiting for us," Eli said, pointing down and adjoining path.

"More walking in the woods, great. Maybe we will run into more big game hunters," Tasha groaned

"This way will be safe. The place you described is on the edge of our land."

"Your land?" Aya said softly.

"The town's land. We border State land, but, from the sound of it, they crossed a line."

"And they put up traps that have to be illegal. I could have walked right into them myself if I was off the path." Tasha was pissed, from the sound of it.

"She threatened to beat them with her bloody stump if she got hurt," Aya smiled.

Eli couldn't contain his laughter and Jett followed. "I would have liked to witness that exchange," Eli grinned.

"Does Ellery know?" Aya looked to Eli for an answer to that one.

"Yes," Eli nodded.

"Aya, I think maybe being a little more specific would help like 'Eli, does Ellery know we were wandering in the forest and talked to two assholes?' is a bit different than 'Does Ellery know that the werewolves are in danger and Eli had ordered them not to go running willy-nilly?'," Tasha added.

"Willy-nilly?" Jett arched a brow.

"Yes, willy-nilly, so, Eli, which question were you answering?"

"Both," Eli said as they rounded the lake. The homes were visible through the trees just up ahead.

"Oh boy," Aya said softly, stopping to catch her breath.

"Aya?" Jett looked worried.

"I'm processing," she said, holding up a hand to stop him from forming a question or saying anything.

"Let me know if you need to have a meltdown."

"Because you are an expert on meltdowns, or because you are and expert on women?"

"I am neither. I'm a guy that sort of likes you."

"Sort of? You sort of like me? Well, then we should get married. That's all a girl really wants is a guy that sort of likes her."

"Is this you having a meltdown?" Jett looked even more concerned. Aya was rational, down to earth, and the one that the other three in their friend group looked to for advice.

"Yes, I'm sorry. I was pretty sure I was handling this in a mature, sensible way. It turns out I didn't believe it. I didn't believe my own eyes."

Tasha had stopped, looking back to where Aya was. "I've got her," Jett called to her.

"If you hurt her..."

"I know, you'll beat me with a bloody stump," Jett countered before she could finish. This time, even Aya was laughing.

"What does Ellery know?" Aya asked, still unwilling to say the "W" word.

"Everything, she's mated to Eli."

"Mated?"

"Yes."

"So, Eli is a..."

"Wolf shifter."

"Wolf shifter?" Aya said out loud.

"Yes, werewolf is a term that is both offensive and inaccurate."

"I really saw Emerald and the crazy ex turn into wolves and fight on the lawn," Aya muttered.

"Apparently so, we didn't know you were watching."

"It was one hell of a show. Ghost?"

"Shifter," Jett nodded.

"Was Emerald always..."

"No, she was bitten."

"By the crazy one?"

"No, the crazy one had stabbed her and left her for dead. Nico bit her to save her life. She would have died if he hadn't."

"Nico is a shifter," Aya wasn't asking. She was just making sure she had it right.

"Aya, most of the people in this town are shifters."

"Why wouldn't Ellery tell us. We have been friends forever, and Eve… oh, does Eve know?"

"Eve knows, so do Jazz and Ellery, and now you two. Ellery and Jazz had one of Ghost's Ex's shift to Human form in the woods in front of them."

"So, watch out for Ex's."

"Yes and no, it's pretty uncommon for a woman to pursue a man that has found his mate."

"Ghost's mate is Jazz?"

"Yes, his Ex didn't mean her harm. She was just curious. She assumed that Jazz knew about shifters, since they had already been…"

"Already been what… oh… you know what… don't answer that. It's not my business."

"Let's just say they were already mated. She just hadn't gotten the full story. Ellery being there when the Ex-girlfriend showed up was an added problem."

"Is this a secret? Are you going to get in trouble for telling me? Are you one of them? Is this part of some sort of government experiment?"

"Which of the questions do you want me to answer?" Jett laughed.

"All of them."

"I'll start with the big one. Yes, Aya, I am one." Jett waited for her to step back or recoil, but she didn't budge. She just waited for the rest of the answers.

"I figured that might be the case."

"You're taking it well."

"No, not really, inside, I'm freaking out. I have had a week to process that what I saw was real. I figured that crazy ex was a Government experiment gone wrong and she had attacked and turned Emerald. Then, I saw Ghost in all is glorious nakedness change to his Human form. Did you just growl at me?"

"Reflex, I didn't like you calling Ghost glorious when naked. I don't like you calling any one glorious."

"Except maybe you, because you sort of like me?" Aya assumed.

"It's complicated."

"Feel free to uncomplicate it," she said, crossing her arms over her chest and cocking her head to the side.

"Here? Now? Don't you want to catch up with Tasha and see Ellery?"

"Right now, you are the one giving it to me straight. Tasha is as clueless as I am and Ellery hasn't bothered to tell us the truth so far. I'm listening. What else is there? What do I need to know?"

10

"Should I start at the beginning?"

"Start wherever you like," Aya said, sitting cross-legged on the path. She knew whatever this man, or whatever he was, was about to tell her was going to be a lot to digest. She also knew he would tell her the truth."

"Billions and billions of years ago, there was a Big Bang."

"Very funny, maybe start a little closer to now," Aya couldn't help but smile.

"Alright, Wolf shifters and shifters in general have always been around."

"We can revisit the shifters in general part later. So, Wolf shifters are more than just legend?" Aya motioned for Jett to continue.

"Yes, most legends are based in some truth."

"Now, you sound like Ellery. She had to be thrilled when she found out."

"She was pretty excited. We live in groups, mainly for safety's sake. Our pack is one of three in the region."

"Moon Valley and Shadow?" Aya knew that Alice was from a town called Shadow and that Eve and her man lived in Moon Valley.

"You are pretty smart," Jett grinned his signature sexy grin, making Aya's mind wander away from the subject and more to the man.

"Yeah, so smart that I have lived in a Werewolf pack for months and not figured it out."

"We were hiding it."

"That's what you're guarding us for, not because we were in danger but because we are the danger?"

"You're not a danger. You were in danger before we came to get you, but Eve might be the one to explain that part in more detail. She was kidnapped and there was a man that was after her and you and your friends were directly affected because of what happened to her."

"But we aren't really in danger now?"

"Not from us or the bad guy that hurt your friend. He is long gone. I'm more concerned with Paranormal hunters right now. They are a threat to all of us."

"You think they are trying to find Sasquatch or werewolves?"

"Both, I'd guess. They saw something over near the Moon Valley land earlier this week. That is why they are here, setting up elaborate traps. We got word today to be careful."

"You're really a guard then."

"We are the Pack's protection: Guards, Security, Rangers, Enforcers, all of the above. We are the Pack's Police force, basically."

"Does this mean Tasha and I don't have to stick close to the house anymore?"

"It means you have to be even more careful. Aya, you wandered into a Hunter's camp. They hunt with cameras usually, sometimes a Dart gun if they are bold. I've heard of other packs encountering Bear traps, but that's a first around here. Those men could have harmed you or assumed you might be what they were looking for."

"Tasha was ready for a fight and, believe me, the girl can fight."

"I do believe that. I just can't have you wandering alone. I can't have my people wandering at this point. "

"Eli said no shifting."

"I know you heard that. We are people, Aya, just people who sometimes shift into wolves."

"Right, no big deal. I bet Ellery is telling Tasha I told you so right now."

"We asked that she not tell you outright when she found out. The Moon Valley crew and the Shadow seven were all mostly human when they were kidnapped. They learned the hard way. They wanted your introduction to the truth to be more organic." Aya didn't know who the Shadow seven or the Moon Valley crew was referring to, but it wasn't the part that she questioned the most.

"Organic, like seeing a wolf fight on our friend's lawn or having an Ex shift because they are curious. There is nothing organic about it."

"You are right but, in both instances, they had a mate to ease them into the idea. Even Ellery had Eli, who took a minute to realize that she was meant to be his."

"Meant to be his?"

"Shifters tend to mate for life, Aya. We are pretty normal: we make friends, we date, we hook-up occasionally. That ends when you meet your mate."

"Nico was rumored to have hooked-up a lot. They said he basically had a harem."

"Not gonna lie, he had a few women he was seeing, until Emerald let him touch her."

"Oh please, one touch and he knew. Now, your spewing bullshit all over the Forest floor."

"It's true. Sometimes, you just know. Have you ever had the sensation when you meet a person that you just know they are going to be your friend for life?"

"Yes, Ellery, Eve, and Tasha, third grade."

"And now look at you. You went with your instincts. You four are tighter than most sisters, but you couldn't be more different. Am I right?"

"Yes, you're right, so Nico touched Emerald and just knew he had the wrong women on the line. Are you saying that he had never touched her before that?"

"When was that last time any of us touched you, Aya? None of the women he was seeing were 'on the line' necessarily. Take Ghost's ex. She knew he wasn't her mate. She was just curious when she heard that one of the humans at Blythe's, that Jazz was his."

"And that was mainly because she was human."

"Same with Cora, she knew Nico wasn't hers. She was a bit more delusional about it than most, so she attacked Emerald, knowing she could kill her. She didn't attack any of the other Shifter woman that he had been dating, so it was probably more the fact that Emerald was a human."

"Dating shifters is apparently dangerous for humans."

"Sometimes, it can get messy but not usually dangerous. Ellery mated Eli with no issue and Ghost's Ex wasn't out to harm Jazz. Both couples are True mated, meaning the Wolf parts recognized their mate. Wolves mate for life."

"My friends are all mated to shifters and Emerald is one now."

"Aya, they all chose to take their mate's bite to turn. Emerald was an exception. Nico couldn't stand by and let her die."

"Did the others really choose to or were they made to?"

"It's a choice for a human. We have strict laws against turning a human, even a mate, against their will. Emerald was unconscious and dying at the time, so the Alpha made the call and Nico saved her."

"The Alpha?"

"Blake."

"I'm going to leave it there for now, okay. My brain can only process so much at once."

"You can ask whatever you want, whenever you want to."

"Thank you for telling me the truth."

"I told you I would."

"Yes, and, for the record, I sort of like you too."

"That might be a discussion for another day, Aya. As I said, it's complicated."

"Complicated because I'm human and you're not."

"More like, so complicated that if you touch me, it might get a lot more complicated."

"I don't know if I should be more frightened by your answer or the fact that I actually understood what you meant just now."

"Do I frighten you, Aya?"

"Yes, but in a good way."

"Tell you what, the ball is in your court. When and if you want to touch me, then I say go for it."

"And if your wolf decided I'm it, that I'm your Forever mate, whatever you want to call it, then what?"

"I am leaving it up to you for a reason. If you decide you want to find out, I'll assume that you already know you'd be okay with that possibility."

"Yes, I suppose I would be… if I decided to make the first move, that is."

"I'd offer my hand to help you up, but I'm not sure your ready to take it."

"You'd be correct. I'm still going to need to absorb what I know now and maybe ask a few hundred questions," Aya said, scrambling to her feet and brushing the dirt off of her.

The truth was that she wanted to be reckless. She wanted to find out what Jett felt like. She wanted to hold him, kiss him, and have him do far more to her. It was the possible Forever part that stopped her. She smiled to herself, realizing it wasn't the Wolf part or the keeping secrets' part that had her hesitating. It was the idea that he thought she might be his forever and she wasn't sure what she felt

"Jett?" Aya said after they had walked in the direction that Tasha and Eli had a while ago now.

"Yes."

"You already know what will probably happen if I touch you, don't you?"

"I am pretty sure, although no one can ever be 100% sure until they try."

"Then what, fireworks, birds singing, what is it that makes someone so sure?"

"I can't say for sure. If I knew the answer to that, I'd already have a mate."

"That's what you meant when you said you wanted a wife?"

"Humans tend to take mating or marriage seriously at first. Most think it's for life, but the Divorce rate is over 50%."

"Wolf shifters don't get divorced?"

"I didn't say that. Not all shifters find a True mate. The fact that our Alpha recently found his helps. Packs seem to have a boom in True matings when a young, single Alpha finds his True mate. It has a weird Domino effect that I can't explain. True Mated pairs have a 0% Divorce rate. but shifters as a species, the rate is 2, maybe 3 %. With those odds, who wouldn't want a mate, a lifelong companion who loved you?"

"You don't love me, Jett. I don't love you either."

"I don't know you well enough to say either way and you can't say you don't love a thing until you really know for sure. You feel something for me or we wouldn't be having this conversation. I know that I love talking to you. I love being in your presence. I love the fact you haven't gone screaming into the woods."

"The night is young and the traps are a big deterrent," Aya joked.

"You're not frightened of me. You seem to like me back. Some describe touching their mate for the first time as a flood of emotions. It could happen to us, or I could be all wrong and we feel nothing."

"I doubt we'd feel nothing," Aya sighed, making Jett smile. She was interested. There was no hiding that.

"Aya, it is your call. We are here. They know we have arrived, so we can go right in."

"They could hear us?"

"Only the last sentence or two and I doubt they were tuned into us and what we are saying. I can hear Tasha scolding Ellery inside."

"I'd better go save her. Jett, when will you be on duty again?"

"Pretty much every day and maybe night, until you decide."

"No pressure there."

"None, go save Ellery. I'm going to talk to Eli."

11

"There you are. Please tell me you weren't hooking-up with Wolfman Jett in the forest just now? It's been an hour."

"Wasn't it you that suggested I hook-up with 'Wolfman Jett' several times in the last week?"

"That was before."

"Before what?" Aya glared at Tasha. Of all of the people in the room, she should be the one who understood prejudice. Her mixed heritage, like Ghost's and his brother's, was evident without looking at their parents.

"Before I found out that they bite."

"They, you mean Wolf shifters?" Ellery was grinning and trying to sound offended at the same time. It wasn't working.

"Yes, werewolves, the whole town is werewolves."

"Wolf shifters, Tasha."

"Same difference."

"No, it's not," Ellery interjected. "Werewolves are Legendary creatures that turn involuntarily on the Full moon and terrorize villages."

"I know the difference. I read the Werewolf 101 book," Tasha snapped back.

"You did?" Ellery asked.

"Yes, right after Emerald turned into a German Shepard and the psycho chick that wanted Nico turned into one too, then Jazz's man, who, by the way, is fine." Tasha glanced at Jazz, who was silently enjoying the show up until then.

"Yes, he is fine," Jazz grinned.

"So, I guess that means Chance, his brother, is also a…"

"Shifter, yes Tasha, Chance is a shifter. Only you can go off track mid-tirade to ask about a guy. Do you want his number?" Ellery joked.

"No, I don't want his number. Just because you think someone is fine and he has a brother who is… woah is all I can say about that one, it doesn't mean I want a hook-up. Although, it has been a while. We don't want cobwebs to gather in my…"

"You need to shut up, Tasha," Ellery yelled. Yelling wasn't Ellery's thing. It was Tasha's thing. So, Ellery yelling got everyone's attention.

"I was just saying."

"Tasha, I know what you were just saying. I thought maybe I'd warn you that they can hear you."

"Who can hear me?" Tasha rolled her eyes.

"The men outside, all of them: Ghost, Eli, Jett, and…"

"Chance," Aya finished before bursting out laughing. It wasn't really all that funny and Tasha wasn't one to get embarrassed, but Aya had held back so many emotions in the last couple of hours, weeks if you count the incident, it was all coming out.

"They can't hear us," Tasha shrugged. "Shifters can't hear everything we said, even if they are listening."

"And they are definitely listening. Ghost is already taunting Chance," Jazz explained. "I can hear them too."

"Oh well, who cares? A man like that knows he is fine. That probably makes him an asshole anyway."

"And now he knows all about your cobwebs," Ellery lost it, bending over she was laughing so hard. Jazz went wide-eyed and stood abruptly in a reaction that didn't make any sense. When Jazz bolted from the room at inhuman speed, it took a second for Aya's brain to catch up with her eyes.

"What's wrong?"

"Oh, she does that all the time. She's pregnant. She's just puking."

"Just puking after breaking the sound barrier. How fast can you all run now?"

"Really fast, if we need to," Ellery said, looking at her two friends. "Before I forget, I have one more important thing I need to say," Ellery said in a whisper.

"What?" Tasha said leaning forward.

"I told you so!" Ellery said, clapping her hands with glee.

"She's right. She did tell us," Tasha shrugged and all was right with the world. The friendship was still strong as ever.

"We should call Eve and yell at her too," Tasha grinned.

"Better yet, I'll invite her here tomorrow. Your homes are almost done. Now that you know, you can move in."

"Is that what was holding up construction?"

"Maybe a little, it's just easier if everyone knows. If Ghost or Eli had to shift to get to an emergency quickly, it would be hard to hide with the houses this close."

"And where does Ghost's brother live?"

"Tasha, you're starting to be as bad as Mary grace is," Aya scolded.

"I'm just asking a question, *Miss I was in the woods with Jett for an hour before I got here.*"

"Fine, you win. I was alone with a man in the woods for an hour."

"And?"

"And the rest is none of your business."

"I thought so."

"You can think what you want. I assume we aren't breaking the news to Mary Grace and Sarina today."

"That would be the Alpha's call," Ellery affirmed.

"El, why did you decide you wanted to be a shifter? You didn't have to, did you?"

"Humans always have a choice. I was not well, remember?"

"The last X-rays were clear."

"They were clear because Eli bit me. The Shifter metabolism heals faster. "

"Like Nico's bite did with Emerald?"

"Yes, she nearly died with the bite. I like what I am, who I am now. I love Eli with everything I am and I want kids, lots of them."

"Are you preggers too?" Tasha asked.

"I'm not sure, but I think maybe."

"Sweet," Aya yelled. "I'm going to be an auntie."

"Slow down. Eli is sure that I am, but I'm going to wait and see. I feel fine and Jazz is sick as a dog."

"Sick as a dog." Tasha made a face, trying not to smile or laugh but clearly failing.

"No pun intended, Tasha. We are wolves, not German Shepherds and, before you ask, no we don't have puppies."

"Too bad, I like puppies. Babies… I'm not sure about babies."

12

"Are we good?' Jett asked as they walked back toward the old Victorian, this time taking the right path.

"Yes, we are good. Talking to Ellery helped a lot," Aya smiled at the man who was with her. Jenkins had come to report to Eli, so he was walking with Tasha.

Tasha was rattling off question after question. Some were inappropriate by human standards. Werewolf sex was something Aya was trying not to think about at the moment. it was hard not to. Since her talk with Jett in the woods, the man seemed even more attractive to her.

"Can I take you to dinner?"

"Tonight?"

"Whenever you want, Aya. I'm free every night."

"You don't have a girlfriend or friend with benefits out there?"

"No, I have no girlfriend that will stalk you, if that's what your concerned about."

"I was just curious. Let's say I am your mate but you have a girlfriend who you were pretty serious about. How does that work? Everybody gets hurt in that scenario."

"I don't personally have a girl I was ever that serious about. Usually, if the woman is a shifter, she has to know there was a possibility that a man would find his True mate and it would end. It works both ways, a man getting involved seriously with a woman and then she finds her True mate."

"So, do all shifters just hook-up and keep it casual until the right one shows up?"

"Not all but some, I have a friend I went to High school with who dated the same woman for seven years before the Mate fever hit."

"And he left her?"

"No, it hit them. I didn't know why there was a delayed reaction, probably because they were like fourteen when they started dating. I couldn't say. There are people who spend their lives researching how this works, but it's not something you can explain."

"Sounds complicated."

"It is, but all you have to understand is sometimes you know for sure you've met the right one, even without touching them."

"So, we touch, hold hands, do more than that and nothing, then we just forget this whole thing?"

"No, I like you. I like spending time with you. We could just date."

"Until you find the right girl and leave."

"I might never find the right girl."

"I'm not sure I'd want to live like that. You fall in love and think this is it and some stranger shakes your guy's hand and he's gone."

"My mother always said the Universe knows best. I trust fate. I have not gotten so involved with anyone that my walking away would hurt them."

"How many women have you said that you thought they might be your mate?"

"One," Jett said seriously.

"One and me, or just one?"

"One, Aya, just you."

"Oh boy."

"I'm not trying to pressure you. I don't want to frighten you. I'm just being honest. I have little doubt the outcome of you touching me. I need you to want it as well."

"Oh, I want to touch you. I'm just not on board with the Forever part. Forever is a long time."

"It is. If it's supposed to be, it will be and if I'm wrong, I'd still like to take you to dinner."

"Tomorrow night would be better. I'm mentally and physically exhausted today."

"Understandable. By the way, all of the guards are shifters and Blythe is half."

"Half-shifter?" Tasha who had apparently heard the entire conversation exclaimed.

"Yes, one parent was human and one was shifter. There is a one in four chance that the child will be born unable to shift, so she is basally human."

"So, Jazz and Ghost's kid might be human?" Tasha asked.

"Jazz is a shifter now. The child will be Wolf shifter," Jett answered as they reached the old Victorian. "Any more questions before we leave you here?"

"No, I'm good."

"I have a question," Tasha smiled.

"What question?"

"What time are you picking up Aya for dinner tomorrow night?"

"Six, if that's okay?"

"That's prefect," Aya said, glaring at Tasha for even asking.

"Wait, I can't flirt with Mary Grace, but you can take Aya out to dinner."

"Stop," Tasha slapped Jenkins' arm "You heard the same conversation I did. Aya might be Jett's mate."

"So, maybe Mary Grace is mine."

"God help the both of you if that's true," Tasha joked. "This Mating thing sounds pretty serious."

"How much of what we were saying did you hear?" Aya whined.

"All of it, I think."

"Great, at least I didn't say anything embarrassing about cobwebs," Aya bit back. Her friend had probably been listening to make sure she was alright, but it still seemed like an invasion of privacy. Aya had assumed that Jenkins could maybe hear, but his opinion didn't matter like Tasha's did.

"Cobwebs?" Jenkins asked and all three of them, Jett included, burst out laughing. "What did I say?" Jenkins asked, making it even funnier.

"Nothing, Aya, I'll see you tomorrow. Jenkins, I see Susanne is here to relieve you. Go check in with the Surveillance crew."

"Yes Sir."

"Call if you need me," Jett told Aya.

"I will."

"She will. Go on, we have gossiping to do. She will be ready at six."

"Tasha, stop. I'll see you then," Aya said, dragging Tasha toward the door to the B&B, glancing back once to smile at Jett.

She was leaning toward just going for broke and touching him. The more time she spent with Jett, the more time she wanted.

13

"I hear you had an interesting week?" Eve strolled into Ellery and Eli's home with a relieved look on her face.

"You could say that," Aya glanced at Tasha.

Parker, the guard on-duty, had driven all of the women, including Blythe and the others, to the new homes. Jazz and Blythe had already taken the others down to the lake, so that Aya and Tasha could see their friend and ask questions without being overheard.

"You both could have said something," Tasha shook her head.

"It was Eve's call and her story to tell," Ellery explained.

"Fair enough. So, let's have it. What's the real story?" Aya asked.

"Short or long version," Eve smiled at her mate, Kingston, and Alice, the Alpha's mate, who had come for support. Alice and Kingston, along with being Wolf shifters, were actually Medically trained in Medical practice as well as therapy.

"Start with the short version. They aren't going to believe the witch's part?" Ellery grinned.

"Witches?" Tasha barked.

"Yes, witches, the real kind with magic and everything," Elery blurted.

"Go ahead, get it out. Say I told you so," Aya smiled.

"I did tell all of you."

"Yes, you did," Eve soothed. "Witches are our allies, mostly. They have put up safeguards against just anyone wandering onto Pack land."

"Wards, they are called wards," Ellery said excitedly.

"Wards are invisible barriers that make you feel like turning around, basically," Alice added.

"So, people don't want to come here. That's smart. So, how are there men in the woods setting up Bear traps?" Aya asked.

"The Paranormal hunters think the warning is a sign they are on the right track."

"Which it is," Tasha snarked.

"Anyway," Eve said, ignoring Tasha's tone, "I was really kidnapped. That part is true. The others in Moon Valley, along with a group of women in the Shadow Pack, were taken as well. We were the lucky ones. Many didn't survive."

"How many... wait... I don't really want an answer. Go on," Aya said, taking a deep breath.

"The whole reason we were taken was because some insane shifter wanted to cash in on Shifter abilities."

"He was trying to take the essence of the shifter and make it into a drug that was temporary," Alice added. "The goal was that the human wouldn't be able to shift but would heal faster and be stronger until it wore off."

"So, they kidnapped humans?"

"Yes, a lot of humans, the packs came to rescue all of us."

"So, where do we come in?" Tasha asked.

Alice was the one to answer. "With what we think was well over fifty humans disappearing in a three-state region, all at the same time, the mad Alpha needed to find a way to keep anyone from looking for them."

"That's where the witches come in, the bad ones, not the good ones," Ellery smiled.

"The witches have always protected the other Paranormal species from being discovered. They erect invisible wards and they can take recent memories and erase them. If a human wanders onto Pack land and sees one of us shift, then a witch can make him forget what he saw confuse him."

"What happened with us was we were meant to forget entire people, meaning Eve," Ellery explained. "The Mind Wipe thing worked for many of the families and friends of the others, but not us."

"Or the others in the 'Witness Protection Program." Tasha was making air quotes with her fingers.

"Yeah, apparently, you all just loved me too much," Eve sighed.

"Some others were affected and then recovered. All of you were not getting better. You were getting worse, except for Mary Grace, who is a whole other story. The headaches, the coma, the near death in the ICU was your brain fighting what the witch did to your memory of Eve."

"So, how are we alive now?"

"A witch named Harlin, she's amazing. She came and unwiped us so we remembered Eve and the headaches went away."

"The Witness Protection Program was the best excuse to take you from your homes. You remember Eve, but outside of the Pack, no one would recall ever meeting her."

"And I thought last week's Werewolf fight on Emerald's lawn was an eye-opener." Tasha groaned.

"Wolf shifter!" everyone scolded.

I'm okay with never going home. Home is where my friends are. This is nicer than I could have afforded, so it's all good." Aya smiled.

"What about the sexy, handsome guy who is taking you to dinner tonight?" Tasha taunted.

"Why don't you run along and stalk Ghost's brother?" Aya glared at her friend but wasn't really angry.

"You have a date?" Eve asked.

"Yes, I have a date. I'm just not sure if I should go."

"Why?"

"He thinks I might be his mate."

"That is more than just a date, Aya. Do you like him?" That was not at all the answer that she thought she'd get from Eve.

"I like him. Liking him isn't the issue, It's the Forever part, the huge implications of even touching the man. I have to think ahead, like forever when deciding if the guy gets a hug at the end of the night."

"But you are still considering going?" Alice smiled.

"Yes, I want to go. I like talking to him. I like being with him. I just don't want to get engaged on our first date. At least. I don't think I do?"

"If he is your perfect match, you will feel it," Eve assured her.

"Then what? Do I tell him go ahead and bite me? Do I want him to bite me? I don't know?"

"You could bite him instead. I bit Kingston first," Eve grinned.

"Somehow, that doesn't surprise me. You were always a little crazy."

"She still is," Kingston laughed.

"Good thing I bit a therapist. Aya, I have known you a long time. You clearly have been told what he thinks and what could happen. You are still considering going out with him. I think you overthink most things. This guy might be wrong, but if he's right, what's holding you back?"

"Nothing is actually holding me back. I'm still going. What if I feel nothing, or what if I feel something and he was wrong and all this is for nothing?"

"That's life, Aya. Remember Jimmy Frolic," Eve reminded.

All four woman made a face.

"Who is Jimmy Frolic?" Kingston asked.

"Aya's prom date from hell. He got drunk, puked on the Dance floor, and still managed to convince Yolanda Marks, his old girlfriend, to take him back that night. Leaving Aya to find a ride home with us."

"How does this apply exactly?" Aya asked Eve.

"Jimmy married Yolanda and they have three kids, a Rescue dog, and are living happily ever after in the suburbs. You can't fight fate."

"If he was just some guy, it wouldn't matter to me."

"He isn't just some guy though, is he?" Alice smiled.

"No, he's a man I know and have known for months. He's a guy I really like and he's a Wolf shifter who apparently thinks I might be his forever. I've never even kissed the man."

"Kiss him then!" all the women in the room yelled at the same time before bursting out laughing.

"You're not helping make up my mind," Aya grinned, shaking her head.

"Only you can make up your mind about this one, Aya."

"You're right. Thank you, Alice. I think, right now, I just want to go swimming. I have a date later."

14

"Ready," Jett smiled, seeing Aya waiting on the front porch of the old Victorian.

"Yes, I didn't know what to wear. My choices are still limited."

"That's fine, you look beautiful," Jett liked what he saw.

The loose jeans and flowing shirt she had chosen did little to hide what he knew was underneath Jett loved her curves. Aya was stunning. She normally had her hair up, but tonight, it was down around her shoulders.

Jet opened her door, letting her settle into the Passenger seat before rounding the front of the truck.

"Ellery said Eli took her to a Shifter restaurant somewhere on Pack land."

"It's actually on Shadow Pack land and we can go there if you like, but I was thinking something else."

"Anything is fine. I'm just glad to be going anywhere. I love it here and I can't wait to have my own place on the lake, but it's been months of thinking I was in danger, sticking close to home, and having an escort."

"You still have an escort," Jett glanced quickly to see her reaction.

"No, I have a date."

"I'm hoping this is more than just a date, Aya."

"I know. I spoke with Eve and Ellery. I realize for Wolf shifters one date could lead to a lifetime."

"Humans are the same. Every Married couple out there had a first date."

"In a way, I guess it's convenient knowing when you meet the right person."

"It can be, unless the pair isn't on the same page."

"Does that happen often?"

"Not often, some still spend a life together. It's hard to explain."

"I'd like it if you'd try to explain."

"Okay, shifters, when they find the one, are in it for life. Its not a life sentence in a negative way, it's… take my parents, they found each other in their early twenties. They mated right away. They are what we call True mated. When one dies, I know the other will follow."

"That's sad."

"In a way, it is sad for us, but for them, they never want to be apart. That's how Blake became Alpha."

"His parents died?"

"No, our Alpha couple was still childless. There was no blood heir to take over. Blake was his second."

"That would be like Nico?"

"Yes, Nico was once the Head of the Guard, the job Eli now has."

"So, the Alpha died?"

"His mate died. She was in a car accident and even her Shifter healing couldn't save her. Our Alpha held on until Blake had stepped up, taking the pack. A pack without an Alpha is chaos."

"They were True mated?"

"Yes."

"I'm not sure the, 'till death do us die together' part is selling the whole Mating concept."

"Having someone you love with that intensity is frightening, I will admit. There are exceptions, Aya. A mother left without a mate will remain to raise her children. Then, there are couples where only one feels the pull."

"How does that work?"

"Like any Human couple: they meet, fall in love, spend their lives together, but only one is driven by the Mating fever."

"So, if I decide to touch you and you feel nothing, we could still date?"

"Yes, Aya, and I already feel something. Feeling nothing would be impossible."

"I'm starting to wish you never told me about this Mating instinct."

"I'm wishing I skipped that as well. I want to be truthful with you, Aya, no more secrets."

"That's fair."

"We are coming up on the wards. It will feel strange."

"Strange, how?"

"Hard to say. Everyone experiences it differently. I did hear some of the human residents say that out wasn't too bad, but coming back into Pack land was not pleasant."

"I have been warned."

Jett had been right. Leaving the Pack's land had felt like a relief. Her chest got tight. She felt nervous, then a flood of relief, making her release the breath she hadn't known she was holding.

"You alright?"

"Yes, that was strange."

"I barely feel anything anymore."

"Shifters feel it too."

"Yes, the witches put it up to keep humans away and tell shifters from other packs they are entering another pack's land."

"Ellery spent her whole life trying to convince the three of us strange things existed that were hidden from us. In a million years, I wouldn't have guessed she'd be right. Now, two of us are Wolf shifters and I'm on a date with one," Aya giggled.

"I'd say I know how you feel, but I don't. I grew up in a pack and have always known witches and wolves existed."

"I think Ellery's conviction over the years that there was more out there is helping us adjust."

"I'm impressed that you both saw Emerald and Cora fighting in Wolf form and didn't run screaming for the hills."

"I would like to see your wolf, Jett."

"When we get back, I'll shift for you."

"Where are we going?"

"You'll see. We are almost there."

A few more minutes and Aya saw exactly where Jett was taking her.

"A carnival?"

"I heard it was coming and thought you might prefer hot dogs and funnel cakes to a sit-down meal. If I was wrong, tell me now and there a nice Italian place not far from here."

"This is perfect. I can't tell you the last time I was at a carnival."

"What would you like to do first: eat, play the games, or go on the rides?"

"Always rides first, eating should be done after, so you don't get sick. The games are fun but rigged."

"I'm pretty sure I can win a few."

"I'm sure you can. Thank you, Jett, this is the best date ever."

"The first of many."

"I hope so," Aya smiled shyly.

"I know so."

15

"I think I'm dangerously close to a food comma," Aya said, leaning back in the seat as Jett drove toward home.

"I was impressed when you ate the third hot dog."

"It was delicious. I love Blythe, but she cooks all healthy meals. A girl needs a sloppy burger or a hot dog or three now and then."

"I like seeing you happy."

"I like being happy Jett, I think it's time."

"Time?"

"I really want to kiss you."

"Is that the food coma talking?"

"No, it's me. I was thinking about what you said."

"Which part?"

"The part where you said who wouldn't want what Jazz and Ghost have or Ellery and Eli. If we can be that happy, why wait? If you're wrong and I'm not your mate, then the sooner we know the better, because I already feel attached and I don't handle break-ups well."

"I like that idea very much, but maybe not while I'm driving."

"Maybe, you're right," Aya laughed. She was happy beyond happy. Just being with Jett on a normal date felt so right.

"We are coming up on the wards."

"I'm ready," Aya said, not knowing for sure what going into the wards would feel like. She wasn't fond of the near panic attack she had on the way out and Jett had indicated it would be worse.

Aya felt a sudden sense of dread. Her heart was pounding, she was sweating, and her breathing was labored. She imagined that this was what a victim in those horror movies might feel when they know they are about to die but don't know where the threat is.

"Stop the car!" she yelled.

"We are almost through. It's not real." Jett sped up.

"Jett, I don't feel it anymore, but I need air."

"I've got you, Aya," Jett said, pulling to the side of the road and running at inhuman speed to open her door.

Aya fell into him. She had already decided to touch him and throw caution to the wind. His arms engulfed her and she pressed her face into his chest.

"Breathe," he said softly, stroking her hair.

"I was ready for it to be bad, but that was terrifying."

"It gets better when you know to expect it."

"I'm thinking I might just stay put for a while before I try that again."

"I'm not upset that we ended up like this."

"Do you always smell this good?" Aya looked up at Jett and smiled.

"I couldn't say. I'm going to kiss you now. "

"Yes, please," Aya stood on her toes to reach him as his arms tightened.

Aya was no stranger to kissing. She liked kissing a lot, sometimes even more than what came after. She was still unprepared for Jett. He took her mouth, claiming it as his. That was what he was doing, claiming her. She felt the rush, that tingling sensation you feel when a relationship is new. This time it was off the charts. She could spend a lifetime kissing this man.

"Oh boy, that was…"

"Good, I hope?" Jett smirked, reveling a dimple on his right cheek.

"Good doesn't begin to cut it. Is this where you say I told you so? I have heard I told you so twice from Ellery."

"I told you I thought maybe you were meant to be mine."

"Yes, you did. You still feel that way, right? I'm not reading this wrong, am I?"

"Now, I'm sure, Aya. You're not wrong. I would like to get back to town before we decide where to go from here."

"Oh, like your place or mine?"

"My place is a Guard house full of six others, now that Ghost and Eli live at the lake."

"And mine is at Blythe's with Tasha, Sarina, and Mary Grace."

"I can call Ghost and tell him we are going to camp out in the house you chose."

"I need to tell Tasha. She will worry."

"So, that's a yes."

"That's a 'hell yes' as Ellery would say."

"I don't want you to rush into this if you're not sure."

"I'm sure I want you. I'm sure I will always want you. I'm sure that two of my best friends wouldn't steer me wrong when explaining the implications. As long as you are sure, I am."

"I'm sure."

"Oh god, I'm one of those heroines that changes her whole life in moment's notice for someone they just met," Aya giggled. "I always made fun of authors who thought that was realistic."

"Maybe, the authors were shifters," Jett said, helping Aya back into the Passenger seat. He didn't want to let go of her, but they couldn't stay on the side of the road like this.

"That is an interesting thought."

Aya had grilled her friends and Alice about matings. She knew the next major decision she had to make was turning or staying human. Jett hadn't mentioned it when confirming he still felt she was his. Just touching him had been a huge decision. The emotions she felt, the connection to him, would have been something she questioned had she not been warned.

This was real. He was real. She was doing this. Her only hesitation was becoming a Wolf shifter. That was a decision she knew could wait.

"Jett?" Aya realized that Jett hadn't gotten into the truck. He was standing with the door open looking into the forest.

"I thought I heard something," he answered with a finger placed to his lips so she would stay silent.

16

The silence was deafening. Aya had always thought that saying was an oxymoron.

It wasn't that Jett had stopped talking. It was the surrounding forest. There was no sound. Aya strained to hear whatever it was that seemed to capture Jett's interest.

"There is something out there."

"Some*thing,* or someone?"

"Not sure, hand me my cell and get into the Driver's seat."

"What… no, you shouldn't be going out there alone. That seems like a bad idea."

"Not investigating is a bad call, Aya. You do know how to drive, don't you?"

"Yes, I know how to drive, but I don't know where we are and I'm sure as hell not leaving you here alone."

"I'm calling for back-up."

"Then, we will wait for the back-up."
"Aya, I can't risk you being hurt."

Aya didn't have time to reply when a horrible animal scream filed the silent night.

"Here, take this, tell Blake what's happening."
"I don't know what's happening."
"Neither do I, Aya. It is my job to find out. Stay on this road until you see a town. That will be Moon Valley. The Alpha is Stockson. It's where Eve lives with Kingston."
"Jett."
"I have to go," Jett said, stripping off his clothing until he was standing in front of her, stark naked and vibrating with power.
"You'd better come back in one piece," Aya said softly. "Go, I'll be fine," she said as Jett, a man who checked all the boxes on her perfect partner list, turned into a large black wolf and ran toward the danger.

"Blake, it's Aya. We are, oh hell, I don't know where we are. We just passed through wards. Jett told me if I go straight on the road I would end up in Moon Valley."
"He left you?"

"He heard something, then something or someone screamed. He shifted to investigate and told me to call for back-up."

"Have you reached moon Valley yet?"

"No, I'm still here. He might need me."

"You need to get out of there. He wouldn't have left you if he didn't think it was serious. You won't be much help unless he already turned you. Are you still human?"

"Yes, it was a first date. I'm reserving changing species for at least the second date."

"He wasn't upset?"

"At what, Blake?"

"Aya, did he run because you rejected him?"

"I didn't reject him. I'm not going to. We stopped because the wards made me sick, then he heard something but I heard nothing. Are you sending help?"

"We are already on our way, but we are twenty minutes out. You said you heard nothing."

"I heard the scream, but before that, it was like no sound, no birds, nothing. Jett heard something. He didn't explain what he heard before the scream."

"Human or animal?"

"It sounded animal to me, but I'm from the suburbs. We don't get a lot of screaming wildlife."

As if on cue, another cry echoed so loudly that she heard it with the doors closed. This one was different, deeper, more of an oooof than an ahhah.

"Blake, hurry, I just heard something else."

"Get out of there."

"Not a chance. What if Jett's hurt?"

"He's trained. You're not." This time it was Alice yelling at her. She had apparently taken the phone from Blake.

"Yes, and I'm human. I know how stupid this is, but I just can't leave him. What if it's the hunters?"

"We have eyes on the hunters you saw. They haven't moved."

"More hunters, then… oh shit," Aya said, looking up from the phone, seeing four huge men standing in the truck's headlights.

*"Aya? "*Alice screeched.

"I have company," she said while smiling and waving.

"Shifter or human?"

"How the hell would I know?" she said, still smiling.

"Say something, like ask what pack they are from."

"And if they are Human hunters?"

"Then, they won't hear you if you're inside the car. Please tell me your still inside the car?" Alice was right. It had been the same idea she had with the hunters in the forest.

"I'm inside, Alice, here goes. Hello, I'm Aya. My… mate, Jett, went to investigate a sound. I'm hoping you four are the good guys. I don't know many people in the other packs."

"Open the door. We are Shadow Pack."

"Alice, they say they are Shadow Pack."

"I need a name."

"Alice wants to know your name."

"Alice, it's Mateo, Axel is with me."

"It's *safe to open the door, Aya. They are safe.*"

"Thank god."

"Tell them what is going on. We are on our way."

Aya was as relieved as she could be, surrounded by four men she didn't know. A female came out of the woods, followed by two more men, as she was telling the first group what had happened.

"How long ago?" the female asked.

"This is Amara, one of the Shadow seven," Mateo explained.

"You used to be human?"

"It's a long story, but yes," Amara smiled

"It's been maybe ten minutes now since I heard anything."

"Start at the beginning," the one named Axel said softly.

"Jett and I were coming back in from dinner. The wards made me sick, so he stopped. The forest was silent but he heard something. I'm not sure what. We heard a scream. He shifted and told me to go."

"Human women never listen." Axel glanced at Amara and she stuck her tongue out at him.

"Don't stick that out unless you intend to use it," Axel said before resuming his authoritative demeanor. "This scream, what direction did it come from?"

"That way. There was a second sound, not really a scream, more like an oooofff."

"Oooofff?" Mateo repeated, pointing to the spot Aya had indicated, and two of the men ran in that direction.

"Watch out for Bear traps and hunters," Aya called.

"Bear traps?"

"Yes, a friend of mine was walking with me and we ran into Human hunters. They are not hunting deer, if you know what I mean."

"That's what Rose meant," Mateo said softly. Aya wasn't sure who Rosé was.

"Rose is Mateo's mate and one of the seven," Axel explained before she could even ask.

"She's also a freakishly good psychic," Amara announced.

"What did she say?" Aya asked, not even hesitating. She wasn't really the type to believe in psychics. That was Ellery's job, but she hadn't believed in shifters or witches either and they were very real. Her sort of boyfriend slash fiancé just poofed into a wolf, leaving a pile of clothing behind as a reminder.

"She said something like westward, a green frog, and a shifter down. We assumed the Western most ward was what was westward"

Aya's eyes went wide as she rushed back to the vehicle, reaching into the back seat and pulling out a huge, stuffed green frog that Jett had won for her at the fair.

"Shifter down, that was the last part," Aya glanced to the dark forest. She wouldn't be able to see a thing once she was out of range of her headlights.

"Jett is out there."

"We will find him," Amara soothed.

"They had cameras, trip lines, and darts," Aya said, hoping more than just the two would follow the trail Jett left.

"Amara, stay with Aya."

"Got it, go," Amara said, watching as the rest of the men ran into the forest.

"What if they have him?" At this point, Aya was pretty convinced that it was hunters that Jett had heard.

"Then, we will get him back."

17

He shouldn't have left Aya. The second he realized he should turn back it was already too late. A female wolf, not a shifter, lay panting on her side, just ahead, and he still couldn't sense any humans or other shifters in the immediate area.

A sharp sting in his side made him falter. Glancing, he saw a dart had come from somewhere off to his right.

Yanking the dart out with his teeth, he slowed, being more cautious in his approach. The dart was making him feel unsteady, but it wasn't enough to take him down.

Whatever drug had been in the dart was more than you'd need to take down even a grizzly. If he was already feeling the effects after just a few seconds, the dose was either meant to kill or it was meant to take down something else.

Even his Shifter healing was having trouble countering the effects. The wolf was not going to live, if she still had a dart in her.

Jett cautiously approached the wolf. She was a wild animal. Even though he was currently in Wolf form, she might fear him.

"I know I hit him," a man's voice came from the direction the dart had.

"Then, why is he still moving?" another male whispered.

"You don't think it is a…" the man didn't finish the sentence, but Jett could smell the fear. Jett might look like a wolf at the moment, but he was a big wolf. All shifters were much larger than their animal counterparts. The small she-wolf on the ground was half his size.

Jett located the dart in her right hind quarters and took it out, hoping it wasn't too late.

He couldn't save her in this form and he couldn't shift at the moment in front of the two, possibly more, men to his right.

Changing direction, he stumbled. He would have liked to think it was intentional, but it wasn't. The drug was still making him feel drunk. As long as he was on his feet, he was probably okay. If he went down, he wasn't sure if he would stay wolf or shift back involuntarily.

If he went down, he might wake up in a lab somewhere or worse, not wake up at all. He couldn't expose his people.

The anger welled in him and his wolf rose even farther in his consciousness. He was being hunted. The wolf and the man were in agreement. It was time to become the hunter and take out the threat.

"Oh shit, Dave, just shoot."
"I can't see where he went."
"There, by the trees."
"We are in the middle of a forest. All there is are trees. I only have two shots left. The rest are in the truck."

Good to know, Jett thought as he slowly and silently crept closer. Two darts were still two too many, but if he could get the Dave character to shoot blindly, he'd have the upper hand.

"I can go to the truck," a third person's voice came from the same direction. Jett didn't know how they had masked their scent originally, but they smelled of sweat and fear now. Three, possibly four, were camped maybe a hundred yards away. Jett paused in the thick brush. He had to think. The wolf wanted to just attack, but the man knew that was likely to end badly.

Four men were no issue. The darts were a big issue. He still felt uneasy and he had gotten it out right away.

These people were looking for big game, big mythical game. The fact that they hit him once meant they had some sort of night vision or night scope on the gun. He wished he had thought to take his pack. If he shifted back to man right now, he'd burn off all of the remaining drug in his system. He would also be naked.

All of the guards were used to pretending to be rangers or local police when encountering humans. The darts they were using had to be illegal. The strength was far more than they would need if they were trying to capture wildlife. If they wanted to kill, they would be using bullets.

"Do you see it?" the whisper on the wind sounded shaky.

"No, if I saw it, I'd shoot."

"Why is it still moving? I thought you said that it would take down an elephant."

"The damn thing took the dart out."

"Maybe, we should go."

"We came out here to find proof."

"Proof of Bigfoot, you said you shot a wolf."

"A giant wolf, bigger than you and me combined."

A shifting of leaves and the sound of heavy footfall heading away from the others was both good and bad. Jett knew that meant less men to deal with, but it also meant that the one moving away could be going for more ammunition.

Jett was pinned down. Even the wolf inside of him had decided that retreat was the best choice, but if he left the thick brush, then he would be seen. If he moved within the thick forest, he would give away his position.

"A giant wolf in haunted woods at night... why the hell did I agree to this?"

"You agreed because if we bring back proof that there's more to this than just legends, we will be rich."

"Or we will be eaten by a giant wolf."

"What if the wolf isn't a wolf at all, Dave, ever think of that? We are out here looking for Bigfoot, so why not a werewolf."

"No, I didn't think of that. I didn't think at all. I honestly didn't think we would find anything. Are you saying you think I just shot a werewolf? If that's what you're saying, I think we might be in trouble."

"You shot it. It's probably just taking longer for it to go down. Maybe, we should go see?"

"Maybe, you should go see. I'm going to stay right here."

Jett was weighing his options. He could wait for back-up, assuming that Aya was able to reach someone. He had faith that his True mate was smart enough to handle anything. If she did what he asked and drove to the Moon Valley Town center, then she was safe.

Jett's experience with Human women had proven that they followed their hearts, not their heads at times. She would tell Blake what happened. There would be help coming. That he was sure of. He had no guarantee she followed his instructions and left.

The more he thought about it, he hadn't heard the truck leave. He hadn't heard much because he was focused on finding the wounded animal and making sure it wasn't a shifter. Now, he was the one in trouble.

The decision was made for him when he heard one of the men coming closer. The brush was thick but not thick enough to hide him from a good night scope. He could see the man, now coming closer, his rifle leading the way.

Jett was left with two choices: one, run away and hope the man has bad aim, or two, run toward him and take him down.

18

Alice and Blake's arrival in far less than the twenty minutes they had indicated had Aya breathing easier. The other men were gone and Amara seemed nice, but they were all Wolf shifters that she didn't know.

"How are you doing?" Alice asked.

"Me, I'm fine. I feel like I should be out there looking with the others, but I can't see in the dark."

"I have a flashlight in my truck," Blake said before opening the back and rummaging through some things.

"I thought he'd say I needed to stay put." Aya said to Alice. "That's why Amara is here babysitting me."

"Blake is your Alpha. I was waiting for orders," Amara shrugged.

"But I'm human," Aya said to the woman she had just met.

"Your mate is Blue Rock. That makes you Blue Rock. Alpha, they went that way, a team of four," she said, turning her focus to Blake.

"Who is Lead?"

"Axel is."

"He ordered you to stay back," Alice smirked.

"I am the only female on the team. It makes sense that I sat with Aya. I didn't take it personally."

"Amara is one of only a handful of female guards in all three packs. Axel is her mate," Alice explained.

"Your mate is your boss.?" Aya asked.

"He is the Alpha second of the Shadow Pack, so yes, he's my boss when I'm working. At home, that's a different story."

Blake motioned for them to follow, handing Aya the light as they went deeper into the wooded area. Aya stepped carefully as the others flanked her.

A distant growl was followed by what Aya thought sounded like a fight. A man was yelling, another actually screaming. The sound had Amara and Blake running, while Alice stayed with her.

"Go, if Jett's hurt, he needs you more." Aya knew Alice was Medically trained as well as being the Alpha's mate and a councilor for the women at the Bed and Breakfast.

"We are nearly there," Alice assured her.

"How do you know?"

"Because I can hear them," Alice answered as Aya started rushing, despite her limited vision.

The thought of Jett being in trouble would have bothered her, even if she hadn't agreed that their kiss was far more than a normal kiss. Love at first sight was just one more thing she hadn't believed in that was apparently very real. Her heart would shatter if he was gone. It didn't have to make sense. It was just the way she felt.

She owed apologies to Ellery and Jazz. She had thought the two of them insane when they moved in with a man they had just met.

A break in the trees revealed her worst nightmare.

Three men were being held by two of the Shadow guards that had shown up with Amara. Amara was checking Jett's pulse as he lay on the ground naked and in Human form. Blake was on the phone barking orders. The moonlight was enough to see the wires and camera set up just past where the Human men were being held.

"What did you do to him?" Aya screamed while rushing the three men, who looked as if they had seen a ghost.

"He is a… he was a wolf."

"You shot him!" Aya was suddenly lifted off her feet as she tried to get to the men.

Her reaction was out of character. She wanted to hurt the men. She wanted to teach them that no one messed with her friends or family and Jett was both.

"Slow down, Tiger, Jett needs you," Blake said, swinging her until she faced away from the men. They aren't going anywhere. I can assure you.

"You are right. Is he alive?" Aya sounded defeated. She felt helpless.

"He is," Alice called from his side. "What is in these darts?" she roared at the men and Aya could swear that one of them wet themselves. A dark stain that might have been just a shadow was blooming down one man's front.

"Horse tranquilizer," one wisely answered, sounding shaky.

"What kind? How much?"

"I don't know," another of the men said before dissolving into tears.

"Alice?" Aya looked at her friend as she knelt next to Jett's head.

"He's alive and breathing. His body is trying to burn off the drug. Stay with him, talk to him."

"Can he hear me?"

"I can't be sure, but if you are his mate, he will know you are with him just by touch."

"Can I move him?"

"He's just unconscious. I don't have anything to counter the dart's effect. Even if I did, I don't know the dose these idiots shot him with."

"He was a wolf, then he wasn't. He's not a man," the hysterical man with the continence problem shouted.

"No, he is a Wolf shifter. We all are, and you three just pissed us off," Blake growled at the man, who then fainted.

The other two were muttering curses and looking terrified.

"I thought there were rules," Aya said softly.

"Remember why we had to come get you?" Alice smiled as Aya settled on the ground with Jett's head in her lap. If Alice wasn't all that concerned, then Aya was sure there was nothing to worry about. At least, that's what she kept telling herself.

"The mind wipe thing?"

"Yes, Blake called in reinforcements."

"Reinforcements?"

"A witch from the local coven should arrive shortly. Those three will wake up tomorrow with one hell of a headache and a healthy fear of dark forests."

"Why would Jett shift?" Aya asked, feeling his breathing even out.

"I'm sure he didn't have a choice. The drug would burn off quicker during a shift. The wolf forced the shift to speed the process. If he was awake, I'd suggest he shift a couple of times to burn it off completely. "

"But he will wake up?"

"Yes, we have an extraordinary metabolism. The drug won't last too long. The shift would just accelerate his healing."

"As long as he's going to be okay."

"I'd say he will be more than okay with you here. I assume your date went well."

"Yes, Alice, right up until it didn't."

"You called him your mate."

"If you had told me even a few days ago that I'd be willing to commit to a man I hardly know after just one kiss, I'd have called you crazy."

"And now…"

"Now, I'm well on my way. My rational, responsible side might need a minute, but my other side wants to jump him and start making babies."

"Believe me, I get it," Alice said, patting her belly.

"You, Jazz, and Ellery, all pregnant?"

"Emerald too, I suspect."

"It's going to be a baby boom," Aya sighed.

"It happens that way when you are True mated."

"Good to know." Aya wasn't sure what True mated was or how it differed from mated, but she felt Jet waking and her attention turned to him.

19

Jett floated in some in-between space. That was the only way he could describe the feeling of surfacing from the deep sleep. The sensation was accompanied by confusion. The only thing keeping him from panicking was a soothing voice assuring him that he was safe.

"I think he's waking up." Jett recognized the voice. Aya was there. She hadn't listened and gone to the Shadow Pack, or maybe she had. He was lost in a fog and not sure of anything.

"Jett, can you hear me?"

The Alpha's voice pierced the fog. Jett was trying to answer. He felt heavy and his words were slurred.

"I'm going to take that as a yes. You were shot with a tranquilizing dart."

"Two," he sighed, not sure if the words were reaching the surface.

"Two?" Alice asked from somewhere.

Jett relaxed, feeling Aya surrounding him. His head was in her lap and she was curled around him. Her scent was comforting, now that he knew she was safe. If Blake and Alice were with them, Aya wasn't in danger.

"Yes, two," Jett sighed. Just those two words had taken all of his energy.

Jett was aware of more people as his metabolism burned off the drugs. His limbs felt lighter than they had at first and he could turn his head to look up at Aya.

"Hey there, how are you feeling?"

"Like I got shot," he managed.

"Twice," Aya shook her head.

"The wolf?" Jett asked as he struggled to sit up. Blake shook his head and sighed.

"She didn't make it. Whatever is in those darts is lethal. You're lucky it didn't stop your heart," Alice growled.

The Alpha female's growl started a chain reaction. A male was crying and begging for his life, somewhere behind where jet and Aya sat.

Reaching over to his mate, he dragged her onto his lap, holding her while trying to make sure the scene was secure.

"There were three," he told Blake when he saw only two huddled together, shaking in the corner.

"The other one passed out. He's over there," a familiar voice made Jett smile.

"Mateo?"

"It's been a long time, Jett, nice to see you. Looks like congratulations are in order."

"I… we… it's…" Jett wasn't sure if Aya was going to agree to being his. The kiss had proven that they were destined, but she was human and might need time.

"Thank you," Aya answered, resting her head against his chest.

"I need to check your pulse," Alice said, coming to sit next to them. "You look a lot better than you did a few minutes ago, but I want you to shift."

"Here, now?" Jett looked at the two men shaking as several of the Shadow Pack's guards hovered over them.

"That ship has sailed. You were in this form when we got here. They saw the shift. The Coven is sending someone."

"Alright, Aya, it's not safe to be to close when I change."

"I will be right over there."

"You were supposed to drive to the Shadow Pack to get help," Jett groaned as Aya extricated herself from his lap.

"I didn't need to. Apparently, a woman named Rose sent them."

"Please, she wasn't about to leave you anyway. Human women don't listen," Axel, the Alpha Second of the Shadow Pack laughed.

"Someone might be sleeping on the couch tonight if he keeps disrespecting my people." His mate Amara wasn't serious and they all knew it.

"Your people are shifters. You're only part human now."

"And I still don't listen, so don't make this about race."

"She's right. I think it's more a female problem," Blake laughed.

"Aya, wait over there. Jett, shift then shift back. That should burn the rest of the drug out of your system. Blake, you and I will have words later," Alice scolded.

"I was just joking, Alice. The Female species is clearly far superior."

"That's better," Alice smiled.

Jett didn't have the energy to stand so he let the wolf take the lead. In Wolf form, he already felt better, clearer. The heavy feeling was fading. Willing the shift back, he stood, testing his Human legs.

"Arm," Alice said, approaching him to take his pulse. "It sounds normal. Do you feel normal?"

"Tired, but I think the drugs are gone, mostly."

"Two of those darts could have killed you."

"I took the first out pretty quickly."

"Good thing, or this could have ended badly," Blake handed Jett a pair of loose pants, then turned his attention to the two men that were still conscious.

"You are lucky my man survived," he said to the two clinging to each other.

"We didn't know?" one of them choked as he sobbed.

Jett looked at the group, wondering what it looked like to a human. Five or six huge men and three women, Aya being the smallest, were hovering around them. They had seen Jett shift. They had heard both Blake and Alice growl and were clearly thinking this was the day they would die.

"You shot an innocent animal and killed her with a drug so strong, it has to be illegal. How would you fair if I shot you with one of these?" Blake asked, pointing to the guns laid out on the ground.

"No, please."

"I'm going to need some answers. Your fate will depend on how truthful you are."

"Yes, yes, anything."

"You three are the second group with a set up like this we have come across. How many are there?"

"Four."

"All have the same set up: cameras, trip wires, traps, and darts?"

"Yes."

"Are you part of a group or just idiots of a like mind?" Axel asked as he motioned for his men to take down the trip wires and destroy the cameras. The cameras were, thankfully, not pointed in their direction and captured nothing.

"It's an On-line society," the second man said with a hint of pride mixed in with fear.

"A society? Explain."

"We want to prove to the world that we are not alone. That humans are not at the top of the Food chain."

"Clearly," one of the Shadow Pack guards muttered.

"I might believe you were trying to get answers so you'd know the truth, if you didn't have lethal weapons and dangerous traps set up on Pack land," Axel approached them, hovering over them.

"Was it your intention to capture us, kill us, or just harm us for sport?" Blake growled.

The acidic smell of fresh urine filled the air.

"We just wanted to prove we were right. We weren't even looking for werewolves. We were looking for Bigfoot."

"Hunting with a camera is one thing but the darts and the Bear trap, along with a trip wire that could hurt an animal running through this forest. That's an attack on our kind. I need the names and locations of the other three sights, the name of this On-line society, and all the information you have about them."

"You'll let us go?"

"I'm thinking about it," Blake stood taller and crossed his arms. "You've trespassed on our lands, violated a member of my pack, and endangered others. Unlike you and your group, we value life, all life."

Jett smiled, wrapping his arms around Aya, as Blake literally scared the piss out of the two conscious men. The third was conscious but pretending to still be out.

"Can I take you home?" Jett whispered in her ear.

"Not yet, I heard the witches are coming."

By Lynn Leite

"You want to stay for the witches?"

"Hell yes, I'm part of this world now. I want to know everything."

20

"It wasn't long before three women who looked like a normal group of women came out of the woods wielding flashlights. The moon had made it easier for Aya to see in the clearing and the god-awful work lights that the hunters had rigged up were now turned on and pointed at them, instead of on some poor, innocent animal caught in their trap.

The trap was gone, the Bear trap confiscated, and the wires removed. The woods were back to normal, except for the makeshift interrogation space as the three humans cowered on the forest floor.

Aya didn't feel even a little bad for them.

"The witches?"

"Yes," Jett said, holding her against his chest.

"They look normal."

"What did you expect, hooked noses and pointy hats?" Jett joked.

"No, I actually expected them to look more like Ellery, flowing clothes and wild hair."

"They come in all shapes and sizes, just like humans."

"But they aren't human?"

"And they can hear you," one of the women smiled as she approached. "Hi I'm Laura and you are."

"Embarrassed, I just never met a witch before," Aya apologized.

"Now, you have. We are human, just extra. "

"Are you born that way? Oh, sorry if I'm being rude. I'm just new to all of this."

"Yes, most of us are born this way. Our abilities are inherited, but occasionally, a human will develop the skills without knowing they had some long-lost witch in their Family history. For someone new to all of this, you seem very comfortable in the wolf's arms."

"This is Jett, he's… he's mine. I recently found out that he was a wolf and that witches existed. By the way, your wards are really working. I thought I was going to die."

"Aya is one of the women that are living at Blythe's," Blake explained.

"Well met, Aya. I have heard you are all settling in well."

"It's been an eye-opening experience in a good way. I'd love to learn more about you and your people. My friend Ellery always believed that you and all of this existed. I'm just beginning to see she was right all along."

"We can do lunch sometime. I like you. You're fun. I have to get to work now."

"You will take their memories?" Aya looked like she was in pain.

"Yes, but it won't be like your experience. You were missing a loved one. These men have known for only hours. They will wake confused and know nothing of what happened here."

"Nice trick."

"It's handy for sure," Laura smiled, joining the other two.

"Did I hear you correctly? Did you just tell the witch that I was yours?" Jett asked, turning her to face him.

"I did," Aya smiled.

"Am I still asking Blake if its alright to head to the Lake house you picked?"

"You need to ask Blake?"

"I want him to sanction our mating. I need him to hear that you want this."

"I want it. I want you. I thought for a second, I wouldn't get a chance."

"I'm here. I'm fine."

"And I'm ready," Aya smiled. "I still need to tell Tasha so she won't worry."

"I think that can be arranged." Jett turned to see Blake and Alice standing together with wide grins on their face.

"Go, I'll call Blythe and tell her you won't be coming home tonight. I think she's getting used to that," Alice laughed.

"Thank you, Blake, I mean Alpha. I fully understand what I'm getting into here," Aya glanced at Jett.

"I can see that. Jett, I sanction the mating and, Aya, if you choose to turn or if you decide to remain human, either way, you are now pack."

"Thank you."

Aya walked beside Jett toward where they left the truck. That had been hours ago. Her flashlight only went so far into the dark woods and the moonlight barely penetrated the canopy.

"If I change, will I be able to see in the dark?" she asked after nearly colliding with a tree.

"Yes, if you want to. It's a big decision."

"Ellery and Eve, both said it was the best decision they ever made. I trust them with my life."

"It has to be your decision."

"Like taking a Wolf shifter as mine 'till death do us part?"

"Yes, like that," Jett grinned

"When Blake said he sanctioned the mating what did that mean exactly."

"It's more of a formality. The Alpha sanctioning a mating means he knows that both parties agree and he is declaring it official."

"So, we are married in the eyes of the pack?"

"There is a little more to it, but yes. We are mated. Think of it like a wedding. The ceremony isn't what solidifies the bond."

"Oh, it's the honeymoon," Aya giggled.

"Yes, the act of love making, the bond we have will be permanent. Again, I have never been mated, but I hear the honeymoon portion is mind blowing."

"I still can't believe I'm doing this."

"We can just take you home until you're sure," Jett assured her.

"No, I'm sure this is right, that you were right, that we are mates. That still seems crazy to my Human brain. I get that your wolf is sure and that makes you sure, but how am I so sure?"

"It's a heart and head thing. When your heart and head are on the same page, it's always right."

"That's a good way to put it. I can't explain how I can feel so much for you in such a short amount of time, but I can't deny it's there."

"The Mating instinct might be a Shifter thing, but humans can feel it."

"If we didn't, you'd be out of luck."

"I'd maybe have to work harder, but I am sure, in the end, you'd always be mine."

"I can't disagree with that."

21

"It looks like Blake might have called ahead," Jett said as they came to the row of houses. It was late but a light shone from the house that Aya had decided would one day be hers.

"I love this house. I was so excited to hear we would still be together. Now, knowing there's no real danger, it's even better."

"You're not sad that you can't go back to your old home?"

"I suppose I could go home now, but my family is already here. Ellery, Tasha, and Eve have been my family for a long time. Now, I have you. Eve being kidnapped and us being mind wiped might have been the best thing that could have happened to us in the long run."

"I don't think a lot of people would see it that way."

"If you focus on life's painful moments, you might miss the beauty in all of the others."

"I think this moment is perfect."

"You don't mind living out here with me?"

"Aya, I live in a home with the other unmated guards. I have a room and the use of a kitchen. Having a home, a mate, and one day, a family of my own is heaven. Most shifters, even though some of the men didn't show it, most want a mate."

"The Mating instinct helps take the guessing out of dating. They are either the one or they aren't."

"The older you are, the more that's true. It can be a delayed reaction or one-sided, but that's rare. Even you felt something for me."

"It confused my Human brain. I'm careful and don't give my heart easily to men."

"Do I have your heart, Aya?" Jett parked in front of the home she had chosen, a home that had been done and waiting for her to figure out the Town secret.

"Yes, Jett, you do."

"Are you nervous?"

"More excited than nervous. I'm scared the bite will hurt."

"We can skip that part. It is your choice."

"I'm agreeing to a lifetime with a Wolf shifter, but a little biting is what has me worried."

"Tell you what, I won't bite unless you ask."

"Alright, being basically married might be enough for one day. Changing species can wait until the morning at least. I try not to make too many life-changing decisions late at night."

"We can wait until morning, if you want to rethink the mating."

"No, I knew when I said I'd go to dinner with you that we would probably end up here."

"You did?"

"Yes, I didn't want you to think I was easy."

"You are perfect. Should I carry you across the threshold? I hear that's a Human tradition."

"You were shot twice and nearly killed tonight. I should be carrying you," Aya giggled as Jett lifted her and entered the home.

"Wow, someone has been busy," Aya exclaimed, seeing that furniture had been added since she was last in the home.

"Blake ordered that all of the homes be done and furnished right after you and Tasha reported there were hunters in the woods."

"Jett, that was yesterday."

"We had all of the furniture ordered weeks ago. it took you girls awhile to figure out that you lived in a Wolf pack."

"Sarina and Mary Grace still don't know."

"If they don't find out on their own by fall, Blake will tell them. The guards are already needed elsewhere."

"Taking down the traps?"

"Yes, you heard that man say it was a whole On-line society. The Moon Valley Pack has Damon. He's a genius. He's the one that found all of you when we realized that some people were dying because of the wipe."

"I'm glad he found us."

"So am I," Jett leaned down, kissing Aya. They had all the time in the world to go over what happened and help find the society. "Tonight, it's just us. Aya, I will always love you. That's the way this works. I will protect you and honor you. This is forever."

"I'm not backing out, Jett. I thank you for wanting to give me that chance."

"I'd hate to wake up tomorrow to an angry Human female."

"We are pretty scary. Take me to bed, Jett. I assume we have a bed."

"If we don't, then the couch looks nice," Jett winked.

Aya was not as experienced as some of her friends when it came to sex. She had always led with her heart and had long-term, sometimes too long-term, relationships.

Jett was the perfect fit. He was kind and patient. He had always had something nice to say, even before she knew he might be interested in her.

Aya couldn't have stopped the fall if she had wanted to. The rush of emotions, the feeling of connection she felt just kissing him was mind blowing. She didn't know if the sensations she was feeing was because he was a shifter and she was meant to be his mate, or if all people felt this kind of soul deep connection when they met the right one?

Jett might be a wolf part-time, but the man slowly driving her insane was all man.

"Jett, please?"

"Please, what?" he smirked as Aya panted, trying to catch her breath.

"I need more," she spoke

"You can have it all," Jett went back to slowly kissing down her neck.

"Too many clothes," she groaned.

Jett was still wearing only pants, nothing else since he had shifted.

"Then take them off." He stepped back, dropping the single item of clothing he was wearing and grinning as Aya didn't hesitate to strip down to nothing.

"And here I thought getting naked that fast was exclusively a Shifter skill." Jett pulled her to him, pressing her into him so the maximum skin to skin contact was achieved.

"I am a shifter's mate."

"Yes, you are," Jett said, resuming his ministrations.

22

The instant they connected in one of the most personal ways a couple could, Aya lost all sense of time and space. She was euphoric. Her brain was on board with her heart and her heart was overflowing. The urge to cry was overwhelming. Never in her life had she been this happy.

"Jett!" She yelled, arching as he sent another wave through her body.

"I've got you."

"Bite me," she screeched.

She needed something more. What it was that she needed was not clear. They were practically the same person they were joined so completely. His body was unreal, solid yet soft. The male body had always been nice but not something that would work her into a frenzy like this. She couldn't get enough.

Looking up to make sure he had heard her, she saw his eyes. They were glowing and had gone more gold than the caramel color they had been.

"I want your bite, Jett," she said to assure him she hadn't just yelled the words. She had meant them.

"I can't take it back if I do," Jett said without missing a beat. Apparently, talking and making her explode at the same time was a skill her mate had.

"I know that. I want to be with you, run with you, have Shifter babies one day. If I'm human, then I couldn't do the last two."

"If you're sure," he grinned, angling his body into a position that allowed his mouth to reach the spot where her shoulder and neck joined.

"I'm sure. Jett, I'm going to explode."

"Together" is all he said before sinking his teeth into her.

The initial sting was brief and the warmth that came after sent her up and over the precipice and shot her into space.

The afterglow was more of an afterburn. Jett held her, his heart pounding and Aya's breathing was slowing. She hadn't said anything, but it wasn't like he could form words either.

"I need sleep," she muttered into his bare chest.

"Then sleep, I have you."

"Yes, you do. Can I shift in the morning? I don't have the strength right now," Aya mumbled making Jett laugh.

"Yes, in the morning."

"You are my husband now, right?"

"Yes, in Human terms, I am your husband."

"Is it too soon to say I love you?"

"No, I have loved you for a while now."

"But you didn't know for sure until you touched me?"

"That's right."

"I'm glad you touched me," Aya said so softly, Jett knew she was fading. He wouldn't have been surprised if she fell asleep mid-sentence.

"I'm glad I touched you too. Go to sleep."

"I am asleep" was the last thing she said before her breathing evened out and Jett closed his eyes to join her.

A loud knocking followed by the sound of a door opening made Jett jump into a fighting stance next to the bed.

"What the hell?" Aya asked, sitting up and rubbing her eyes.

"I'm coming in," Ellery's voice called.

"It sounds to me like you are already in. You shouldn't break into people's houses," Aya yelled, seeing Jett's tense stance relax.

"I knocked and the door was open."

"Open or unlocked?" Aya yelled, kissing Jett before she started searching for something to put on. "Sorry about this," she shrugged.

"She's family. I get it."

"I can hear you," Ellery yelled up the stairs.

"We will be right down."

"I just thought you'd like some breakfast or lunch, since its one o'clock in the afternoon."

"We were up late," Aya said as she descended the stairs with Jett following.

"I'll bet. So how was it?" Ellery asked.

"Which *it* are you referring to?"

"Let's start with dinner. The bite on your neck tells me all I need to know about the end of the night."

"I'm going to hunt down Eli and let him know what happened last night." Jett kissed Aya in a way that wasn't polite in front of company. Good thing Ellery wasn't company.

"Blake called, but I'm sure he'd like to hear the whole story," Ellery called to him as he left. "So, other than hunting hunters in the dark forest, how was the date?"

"It was perfect. We went to the carnival."

"Oh, he's good. How did he know you love carnivals?"

"I have no clue. He's practically perfect. Maybe, he's a mind reader."

"Don't laugh. It's possible."

"Speaking of what's possible, I met some witches," Aya taunted.

"No, you didn't... tell me everything," Ellery leaned in to listen.

Aya told Ellery about the witches, the wards, and the hunters. She confided in her friend that, when she first saw Jett, she thought he was dead and her heart nearly stopped.

"That's the Mating pull. Some Human scientists would say it was pheromones or something, but I think it's magic," Ellery grinned.

"I'm not going to argue that. You were right all along. I'm living the impossible. I might even help you look for fairies, if you want to."

"No, the fairies are in a different dimension or something. I don't think we would find any on this side."

"See, that makes no sense to me, but I'm taking your word for it."

"I'm glad you're safe."

"Oh, that's another thing I failed to mention. The Shadow Pack guards showed up right after Jett left. I had literally just called Blake and Alice was still on the line."

"How did they know you were there?"

"That's the part you're going to love. One of the guards, Mateo, has a mate, one of the original seven that wandered on to Pack land after escaping."

"Go on."

"She said something about Westward, a green frog, and shifter down. There was more to it, but I was on the Western edge of the land. Jett was definitely down when we found him."

"Green frog?"

"Jett won me a giant green frog at the fair. It's still in the truck. Rose, that's her name, is the Pack Prophet. She sees the future. It's right up your alley."

"Amazing, so they found you because a psychic told them you'd be there."

"Apparently." Aya was happy to have her friend living so close that she could pop in and bring breakfast, but she wanted Jett to come back soon.

By Lynn Leite

He had been gone less than a half hour and hadn't gone far, but she missed him. He evidently felt the same, since the moment Aya and Ellery went out front to enjoy the fresh air, he was there with Eli, sitting on a bench near the front door.

23

For the next three days, Jett barely left her side. They ran as wolves. They ran as human. They made love under the full moon. It was common for newly Mated shifters to spend days together as part of the initial bonding. It wasn't just a honeymoon.

"I have to go to work today. Do you want to stay here or go to see Tasha?" Jett asked.

"I'm not sure. I will figure it out," Aya said, dressing for the heat. The day was going to be a scorcher. "I'll probably stay here since the lake is the place to be on a day like this."

"If you go to Blythe's, take the truck. I don't want you walking in the woods right now."

"Are the hunters still a problem?"

"Yes, it's still early in the Summer season and this society the men mentioned has targeted the area as being prime hunting. There's a huge reward for proof of bigfoot."

"What about proof of Wolf shifters?"

"I'm sure that would be an added surprise. We are making sure that they at least lose the Bear traps. Some of the camps are on State land, so we don't have the jurisdiction."

"Can't you call the state?" Aya asked, knowing that Bear traps had to be illegal.

"Yes, we can, but then the state would be wondering why so many humans thought something was out there to hunt. We can't really afford the state getting curious and sending the EPA to find a new species or something."

"Can the witches make them forget why they are here and send them home?"

"Witches live by a code of ethics. Wiping a hunter's minds of certain events to save three packs of shifters from harm and hide their people as well is one thing. Wiping them and changing their minds when they didn't see anything and can't expose us is morally wrong."

"I can see that."

"Other than the wards meant to make them choose to go, the witches will only step in if our kind is exposed."

"Do no harm."

"Exactly."

"Then, who wiped my mind so they could kidnap my friend?"

"Not all witches are good, like humans and shifters are not all good, Aya. The witch responsible for all of you being wiped is gone."

"Gone?"

"I believe they took her power and imprisoned her."

"Took her power, how?"

"I couldn't say. You have to ask a witch."

"Laura said we could have lunch sometime. Do you think she was serious?"

"I think she saw the kind, generous, loving person that we all see, Aya. I'm sure she will contact you at some point. I don't have the witches on speed dial or I'd say you should call her."

"You can never have too many friends. Go to work. I'll call if I go to Blythe's."

"And you will drive?"

"Yes, I will drive there."

"Love you."

"Love you too," Aya smiled, watching Jett walk out the door and into the surrounding forest. Just walking into the forest was a weird commute, but they were Wolf shifters.

As promised, Aya took the truck to the Bed and Breakfast with Ellery coming along. Tasha waited at the top of the stairs with an I told you so look on her face.

"Four days ago, you left on a date and I haven't seen you since."

"I called," Aya smiled, knowing Tasha was not really upset.

"So, do you have to find a man to be allowed to move into the Lake houses, or can I stay single?"

"I thought you were interested in Ghost's brother," Aya reminded.

"I'm interested in hooking-up, not committing for life. No, thank you. I just want to clear the cobwebs," Tasha said in a serious tone, making them all laugh.

"I'm sure you can move in," Ellery finally said after catching her breath. "Your house is done and you know stuff."

"I do know stuff," Tasha smiled. "I even read up on 'stuff' since my friends have abandoned me."

"Oh please, if you found someone to deal with your cobweb problem, you'd ghost us. Get it. Ghost is his brother," Ellery chuckled.

"Very funny."

"Give it a *Chance*... get it," Ellery laughed even harder.

"You are in rare form today," Tasha smiled, seeing Ellery so happy, even if her friend was making Tasha the butt of all her current jokes.

"I got some news," Ellery beamed.

"You're pregnant?" Aya said, seeing that she had guessed right when Ellery started nodding. "I'm so happy for you."

"Babies? You are all having babies. Maybe, I'll stay here with Blythe for a bit," Tasha whined.

"Oh please, you love kids," Ellery scolded.

"I love kids, the kind that can talk and walk, that can dress themselves. Babies are different."

"Oh, so Auntie Tasha only does toddlers."

"That's right. Like Emerald's kid, Gwen. She is so cute and sassy."

"It's her sassiness you like?"

"Yes."

"Are you saying that you're not planning on having children one day? It's probably different when they are your own."

"If and when I decide to commit to a man, as in probably never, he will have to do diapers, wake in the middle of the night, and clean up the spit."

"You know we are joking, Tash. If you don't want kids, don't have them. Just watch out, these Shifter men are apparently really fertile."

"Since I have no man, and the one I had my eye on hasn't been around, I think I'm safe for now."

"Chance doesn't seem the change the diapers type," Aya said, looking at Ellery for confirmation.

"You've seen him?" Tasha's whole face lit up.

"No, we just wanted to see your reaction," Ellery smiled.

"So what? I have a crush on the big guy. That doesn't mean he's interested in me."

"He could be your mate."

"Shut your mouth. I'm staying single and childless."

"As long as you are happy." Aya was sure that Tasha would benefit from a partner, but she wasn't going to push the issue.

24

Did you notice that Mary Grace looked sad?" Aya asked Ellery as they drove back to the Lake Shore houses.

"I did. That girl has a lot going on. She has a twin sister she didn't know she had. She has an Ex who nearly killed her more than once. She is scolded daily that she's flirting too much."

"Tasha is hard on her, but she is playing with fire. Her track record with men is bad. Look at the way she is with Jenkins."

"Jenkins isn't that bad. Eli says he is one of the best guards and would take a bullet for anyone here in the pack. He's just sort of obnoxious."

"He's overconfident and all over Mary Grace."

"She's sweet and receptive. I'm sure its innocent. He wouldn't hurt her, if that's what you're worried about. It's the first thing I asked Eli."

"There are many ways to hurt a person, El, and it doesn't have to be physically."

"True, but the shifters seem to have a sort of code of honor."

"Unless you're a stubborn, Psycho Ex and hate humans. Remember what happened to Emerald?"

"I doubt that's the case. I will mention your concern to Eli, if you want."

"No, I'm just looking out for Mary Grace. She's so naive. Didn't you notice how quiet she was today?"

"I think she is lonely. She doesn't get along with Sarina the way she does with us. Now, you, me, and Jazz have all moved out. Tasha mentioned that her house was done too. She's sad that we are all moving away."

"We are moving to a place that she will live in too as soon as she finds out the Town secret."

"I feel like just telling her."

"That is not our call, Aya."

"I know, maybe we can bribe Jenkins and ask him to shift in front of her, by accident of course."

"Of course, you're not usually the one who comes up with the devious plans." No, I'm not, but I want all of us together. I feel like I moved out, leaving family behind."

"I felt the same way, then you and Tasha figured it out."

"We saw undeniable proof and I still didn't believe it at first."

"And now you're a Mated shifter in a Wolf pack protected by witches."

"You enjoy reminding us of just how right you were."

"I was actually hinting that you might introduce me to your Witch friend, what's her name?"

"Laura, but how…"

"Shifter hearing… I heard you on the phone. Are you allowed to invite a friend to launch?"

"I'm not sure, but I will ask."

"Thank you."

The moment they started down the narrow road that led to her new home, Aya felt like she was home. She was getting used to her wolf and the strange feelings she had when the wolf's personality rose to the surface. If she had to explain what being a shifter felt like, it would be like she had a little voice in her head that helped her make decisions. Not the kind of voice a mentally ill person might have, but one that was a part of her, just in a different form.

"Are we late?" Ellery asked, seeing Jett was waiting along with Eli.

"Not that I know of," Aya shrugged.

"Eli, is everything alright? I thought you were working," Ellery jumped out of the car as soon as Aya parked.

"We got done early. The hunters are all off Pack land thanks to an order from the Mayor's office."

"You mean Blake," Aya said, walking into her mate's arms."

"The witches have added a little more to the wards. We should be good for a while," Jett smiled, knowing just how badly Aya had felt when they went through the wards.

"They added more! Remind me not to leave Pack land."

"Your wolf would make it easier for you to get through."

"I have no reason to leave. I have everything I want right here."

"And on that note, I'm going to make my mate dinner," Eli smirked.

"Are you cooking dinner for me too, Jett?" Aya smiled at her mate.

"If you want me to, I will. Just be warned, I'm not the best cook."

"In that case, I'll do dinner," Aya laughed as Jett took her hand and they walked into their shared home.

"I do have some ideas for dessert," Jett's words dripped with innuendo.

"I am a firm believer that part of being an adult is that you can choose dessert first."

"Dessert first it is," Jett beamed at her.

"And second and third," Aya giggled like a kid as she raced up the stairs.

"Have I mentioned lately how lucky I am that I found you?"

"I'm the lucky one. If you hadn't had your Mating instinct go off when you did, it might have taken me years to realize you and I were a perfect match."

"You had the faith to, at least, believe in the possibilities."

"I'm a big fan of possibilities. Are you getting naked, or do you need my help?"

"First one naked gets the top," Jett smiled, unbuttoning his shirt one button at a time slowly, instead of pulling it over his head.

Aya took the hint, stripping with almost Shifter speed and waiting as Jett caught up.

"Are you happy with our life, Aya?"

"More than happy, Jett, I have everything a woman could ask for and some things I didn't know existed."

"You mean your wolf?"

"Yes."

"Do you regret the bite?"

"Not at all, I love running in fur and in skin. She's part of me, maybe the best part."

"I'll show you the best parts," Jett growled, falling back onto the bed, taking her with him.

"And here I thought you loved all my parts," Aya teased.

"I do and to prove it, we can have dessert both before and after dinner."

"I love a man with a plan."

If you enjoyed reading Aya and Jett's story, please consider leaving a review? Reviews are the life's blood of the independent author.

<u>Wolf Man</u> is Book 5 in the Blue Rock Shifters series. Who's next? I'm leaving that as a surprise for now.

I appreciate all of my readers and would love to hear your opinions, good or bad. You can find me on my Facebook page, Paranormal Twist, for information and updates and to see what's next.

Other series by Lynn Leite:
Moon Valley
Pack
Dragon Fire
Undying
Ridgeland Bears
Howlin Ranch
Shifted
Bitten
Ascension
Spark
Omega
Sierra Moon
On Tour (A contemporary romance)

You can find these and other stand-alone books on Amazon. As always, thank you for reading. Your ratings and comments are much appreciated.

Happy reading, Lynn Leite.